Internal Memo: C
From: Mayor Patrick O'Shea
Re: Increased funding to emergency services

The recent aftershock that struck Courage Bay has brought home to me once again the urgency in gaining council's approval for increased spending for the city's emergency services.

As you know, I spent many years as a firefighter for the city, but never before has the need for extra funding been illustrated so clearly to me as the night of the aftershock. My administrative assistant, Briana Bliss, and I spent almost ten hours in a disabled elevator waiting for rescue. We requested that we be placed on low priority because we knew we were in no immediate danger. However, as you know, not all citizens of Courage Bay were as fortunate that night.

It is my belief that extra funding to our emergency services would result in quicker response times and a decrease in casualties. This past year has been a tough one for our city. We've had storms, forest fires, earthquakes and mudslides.

The police, fire and medical services have all been pressuring the city for larger budgets. It is hard for me to understand how anyone who loves this city as much as I do could think twice about increasing the funding. If we delay any longer, more lives will be lost. Now is the time to act.

About the Author

NANCY WARREN

got her big break when she won Harlequin's Blaze Contest in 2000 and then sold three books for three different lines. Nancy has since written more than a dozen books for Harlequin Blaze, Temptation, Duets and special projects. She also writes bigger books for Kensington Brava.

Nancy lives in Canada with her husband, who has become a romance reader and fan, and her family, who have learned not to ask "when's dinner" but instead are learning how to cook. She has recently taken up Pilates and has the sore abs to prove it!

NANCY
WARREN

AFTERSHOCKS

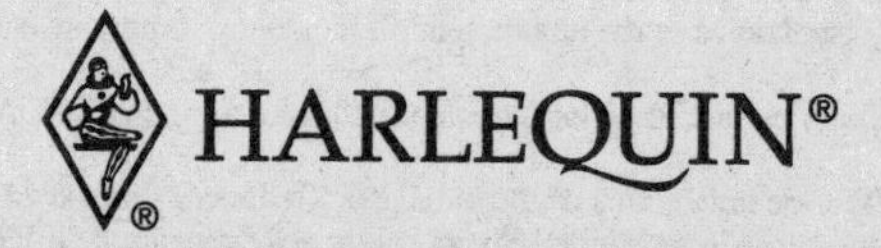

TORONTO • NEW YORK • LONDON
AMSTERDAM • PARIS • SYDNEY • HAMBURG
STOCKHOLM • ATHENS • TOKYO • MILAN • MADRID
PRAGUE • WARSAW • BUDAPEST • AUCKLAND

HARLEQUIN BOOKS
225 Duncan Mill Road, Don Mills,
Ontario, Canada M3B 3K9

ISBN 0-373-61291-5

AFTERSHOCKS

Nancy Warren is acknowledged as the author of this work

This edition published by arrangement with Harlequin Books S.A.

www.eHarlequin.com

Printed in U.S.A.

Dear Reader,

This is my first ever continuity, and I have to say it's been a wonderful experience. As an author, I found it a real challenge to write about characters I hadn't created and a plot that wasn't my invention, but the minute I "met" Patrick and Briana, I knew we were going to have some fun together.

The other thrill about doing Code Red was having a chance to work with authors I love, whether they normally write for Intrigue, Superromance or Blaze. It was a fun, supportive group. I hope you enjoy your time in Courage Bay as much as I enjoyed mine.

Hearing from readers is one of the best parts of my job. If you'd like to drop me a line, enter my contest or have me send you an autographed bookplate and a bookmark, come visit me on the Web at http://www.nancywarren.net.

Happy reading,

Nancy

CHAPTER ONE

PATRICK O'SHEA wanted the one thing he couldn't have.

The knowledge burned inside him from nine in the morning until five in the afternoon every weekday—which were the hours his admin assistant, Briana Bliss, worked, plus a whole load of overtime.

It was Briana he wanted. Even admitting to himself how badly he lusted after her was dangerous. She was out of bounds. Verboten. Untouchable.

Yes, untouchable. And he wanted to touch her so badly that their constant proximity was torture.

The last time he'd wanted a woman this badly he'd married her. Patrick glanced at the picture on his desk, at the smiling face of the woman he'd loved faithfully for more than a decade, including the three years she'd been gone.

"Are you laughing, Janie?" he asked softly, tightening his tie and slipping on his suit jacket. At first when he'd started talking to the framed photo, he'd thought grief might be making him insane, but now he realized it was his way of staying in touch with his memories. Janie's laugh had been light and quick, and he imagined she'd laugh now if she could see him.

Here he was, finally registering signs of vitality in that

part of his anatomy he'd thought had died with his wife, and the woman who'd brought them rushing back was the one woman he couldn't have. Not without going against his principles and destroying his career, his credibility and his reputation.

"Honey, you never should have left," he told Janie, knowing that he'd never have thought about Briana sexually if he were married. Janie knew it, too.

She'd been a warm and generous woman who would never want her children to remain motherless for long—or her husband a widower.

"Maybe this is a sign I'm ready to look around? Maybe lots of women would get to me this way?"

Janie didn't reply, merely stared back, forever young, forever smiling.

A soft knock sounded, and the oak door of his office opened. He didn't have to turn to know who had entered. Every male atom in his body—and they were all male—quivered to attention.

He turned and, even though he'd known it was Briana, was still slammed by the force of attraction. God, she was beautiful. Blond and green-eyed, she had a generous mouth and a determined chin. Her blouse wasn't tight or revealing, yet her spectacular curves made it seem both. Her skirt was straight and hung to below her knees, but he had enough imagination to sketch in what couldn't be seen.

At six foot three, he was used to looking down on women, but Briana was tall. Six feet, probably, when she wore those sexy high heels he loved. Like the ones she had on today.

"You've got to hurry," she told him with a quick smile.

"Don't want to keep the chief of police waiting for his dinner."

"I hope Max is more worried about how to make this city safer than he is about what's on his plate," Patrick grumbled. Still, he patted his pockets rapidly to make sure he had his wallet, then grabbed his briefcase and headed for the door, holding it so Briana could pass through ahead of him. She stopped to pick up her shoulder bag on the way out, which meant she was going home, too. Good. Too often, it seemed, she worked more hours than he did.

The scent of her reached him. Not her perfume—he didn't think she wore any—but some kind of skin lotion that smelled like the sea air out here in Courage Bay right after it rained. Clean and fresh and bracing.

The scent wasn't remotely sexy, but it turned his libido inside out. He shook his head as he shut the door behind him. The door didn't fit perfectly into the frame and he had to shove it with his hip before he could lock it—one more reminder of last month's earthquake. The way things were going, he doubted the city would ever get around to fixing the minor damage done to city hall. The mayor's door was definitely at the bottom of the list.

At the top of Patrick's list was increasing emergency crews and bettering response times. That's what he'd be discussing over dinner tonight.

He glanced at Briana's swaying hips as she walked ahead of him on those perky heels, and he wished like hell he was having dinner with her. The conversation would be a lot more fun, and so would the view. And then, maybe afterward…

He shook his head as though he could shake his fierce

attraction right out his ears. The rash of disasters and tragedies that had struck his town in recent months ought to have him thinking of something other than sex, but somehow, the added stress of being mayor of Courage Bay, California—which ought to be renamed Bad Luck Bay—hadn't lessened his desire for his assistant. As disaster after disaster struck, he'd worked grueling hours, and Briana had worked right alongside him.

You learned a lot about a person during times of stress, and what he'd learned about Briana was that underneath her megababe exterior was a focused, quick intelligence and a sentimental heart.

She was, in fact, as fine a person on the inside as she was on the outside.

Patrick normally ran down the three levels of stairs from his office to the main foyer of city hall, but a glance at those heels Briana was wearing had him punching the elevator button.

She was holding the printout of his schedule for tomorrow. "Depending on how your dinner goes tonight," she said, tapping her pen against her chin, "I can free up some time tomorrow for a press conference if you need it."

Patrick snorted. "You have more faith in my powers of persuasion than I do. Max and I will talk and argue. We both agree we need more manpower, but I've got a budget to worry about and a council to convince." He rubbed the back of his neck, feeling the knots of tension there. "I'll call you if…"

No, he wouldn't. Calling Briana at home, at night, was emotionally pathetic and politically asinine. "Scratch that. If a press conference is necessary, which I doubt, I'll call Archie—he's the media guy. He can pull together a scrum."

The elevator whirred to a stop and the doors slid open. Patrick sent a semidesperate glance down the corridor, only too happy to hold the elevator for anyone—anyone at all—but not so much as the tip of a shoe showed. The corridor was empty, the floor quiet. As usual, he and Briana had outworked the rest of the staff.

Normally, he avoided being alone in closed spaces with Briana, partly because he didn't want to torment himself unnecessarily. He was no more of a sucker for punishment than the next guy.

But there was another reason.

Patrick had been sick to his stomach last year when he saw the grainy footage on the TV news station of then mayor Herman Carter—the *married* mayor—getting it on with his admin assistant in a sleazy motel.

After the footage aired, the assistant slapped him with a sexual harassment suit, Carter's wife filed for divorce. His inappropriate behavior cost the man his job, his marriage and, according to local gossip, most of his money.

Not that Patrick wanted to benefit from another man's misfortune, even if it was self-inflicted, but that sex scandal had eventually led to Patrick himself getting the mayor's job.

He'd been fire chief then, still grieving the loss of his wife and questioning a lot of things. He knew he'd spouted his mouth off a little more vigorously than he might have had he not been furious that a man with a living, healthy wife would screw around, while Patrick, who'd barely peeked at another woman in all his years of marriage, should lose his young wife to a sudden brain aneurysm.

He and Briana stepped into the elevator and he took up

a position behind and a step away from temptation. To a stranger, his rapt attention might appear to be on tomorrow's appointments, but really, he was mesmerized by the blond fall of hair, the way it curled provocatively against her cheekbones and teased her jaw.

How much more of this could a red-blooded man take?

"Why don't you let me put in a word for you tonight with Max?" he asked. "The police department has far more challenging positions than anything I can offer you. I hate to see you wasting your talents on scheduling my speeches to the rotary club and presenting service medals to school kids. You're overqualified for what you're doing." Indeed, he'd been amazed that she'd applied for the job. Before coming to Courage Bay she'd been the city manager of a small town in the Midwest. She was so much more qualified than the other applicants that he'd been grateful she was even interested in the position. He still was grateful to have her working with him—except it meant he couldn't ask her out.

She glanced up, startled. Probably he'd sounded more vehement than he'd intended. He could have sworn a light blush warmed her face. As he gazed into her bright green eyes, intense sexual awareness passed between them—and not for the first time. He couldn't come right out and make his position clear—that he wanted her to take a promotion so he could ask her for a date—but damn, he wished she'd take the hint.

As usual, she didn't.

Her lips tilted slightly and she glanced away, as though denying the attraction that hovered in the air. "Are you trying to get rid of me?"

"You know I'm not." Quite the opposite. For a very smart lady, Briana was acting pretty dumb. Or else she simply wasn't interested in him, and all those sizzling glances were the product of his overheated imagination. He was so out of practice with women, he wouldn't be a bit surprised.

A slight shudder ran through him. He'd pledged the people of Courage Bay his integrity and his morality and he took his promises seriously. Getting involved with an employee was a bad, bad idea. Getting involved with his admin assistant would be like taking a gun and shooting himself in the foot.

He wanted to touch her so badly he had to shove his fisted hands in his pockets.

She passed him a computer printout and he was forced to take the thing. "What's this?"

"I ran some numbers for you. If Chief Zirinsky starts throwing statistics at you, you'll be able to check them for accuracy."

He chuckled. "A cheat sheet."

She shot him a glance of shock. "I can't believe you'd even know that term." She widened her stance and dropped her voice, slowing her usual quick speech. "A man is only as good as his ethics."

Since it was a favorite saying of his, he had to assume she was imitating him. Still, her teasing only reminded him that he'd allowed his campaign team to hoist him onto a damn white horse. A Mayor with Morals had been his slogan. Now he had to live with the consequences.

While he scanned the stats, trying to concentrate, he was keenly aware that he wanted to bury his nose in Briana's hair, run his lips down the curve of her throat—

Abruptly, all visions of Briana fled from his mind, and it wasn't the rising number of suspicious homicides or the increasing delays in 911 response times that grabbed his attention.

It was the lurch of the elevator. It banged and shuddered like a children's carnival ride, throwing Briana and Patrick against the back corner. He hit first, jarring his shoulder against the faux wood panel. Instinctively, he put his arms out to brace Briana when she landed, with a sharp cry of panic, against his body.

He held her tight against him, then dragged them both to the floor, rolling her on top of him. With only two floors to drop, there was a good chance she'd survive, especially if he cushioned her with his body.

She didn't argue, or struggle, but let him maneuver them until her body pressed his from breast to ankle. Like lovers.

They clung together while the world shook and trembled around them. Each second seemed like a year. After the earthquake last month, he knew the signs well. Was this going to be another major quake or a milder aftershock?

First came a shudder, then a rumbling noise as the elevator swayed and their bodies rolled back and forth like surfers waiting for a wave.

He held her tight against him, every muscle and nerve tensed for the cable to snap and the elevator to plunge.

Then, as suddenly as it began, it was over. The thunderous noise stopped. The elevator stilled.

The cable had held.

Still, they remained unmoving, pressed together. He heard the thump of her heart, felt her body so soft and womanly against his.

"Aftershock," she whispered, her breath soft against his ear. He heard the tremor in her voice, and felt it throughout her body, but she had herself in control. She wasn't going to scream or freak out on him.

"Nothing too serious," he said softly in the same tone he used to soothe Fiona, his five-year-old daughter.

"Are we out of danger?" she asked, rising up on her elbows to stare down into his face.

He grinned up at her. "I think so."

Relief made him light-headed. His kids weren't going to lose him. He was alive, healthy, reasonably young, and it looked as though he and Briana were going to see another day.

He was also lying beneath a warm, wonderful, sexy woman.

"You okay?" he asked, running his hands up her arms and lightly over her back.

She made a sound in the back of her throat and he felt a shiver run through her that had nothing to do with fear.

Her gaze was locked on his, the clear green clouding with passion. Her lips, soft and full, opened slightly in a silent plea.

His own body hardened immediately in response to the expression in her eyes and the press of her body against his. Their minds might have dozens of reasons why intimacy was a bad idea, but their bodies didn't care.

Patrick thrust his hands into her hair, pulled her head down to his and kissed her. He couldn't think of a better way to celebrate life.

The heat that flared between them was amazing. Hotter than he could have imagined. With a soft sigh, Briana flicked her tongue into his mouth, making him half crazy with excitement.

It was as though all the electricity that surged between them was too much for the city's power grid. As he deepened the kiss, pulling her even closer against him, they were plunged into darkness.

CHAPTER TWO

BRIANA CLOSED her eyes. Not that it changed anything. They were trapped in a pitch-black elevator, and she couldn't see anything whether her eyes were open or shut.

But closing her eyes was an automatic response to the passion roaring through her system. She wanted to hold it to her, shut it in tight, let it bubble and boil behind her eyelids.

She wanted Patrick to kiss her and keep on kissing her.

She'd wanted it for weeks.

But she'd never imagined anything could feel so good.

So lost was she in the sensations of his lips moving on hers, his hands in her hair, his body hard and muscular beneath hers that she almost forgot her purpose. The one thing she'd strived for in the two months she'd worked here.

Her purse had tumbled from her shoulder when Patrick had thrown them both to the floor. Hanging on to a thread of sanity, she groped around and found her bag. Slipping a hand inside, she automatically identified objects. The rectangular smooth item was her wallet, the flat metal object was...no, that was her cell phone. Her fingertips continued to search even as desire built within her.

Ah, there. Larger, wider, metal. Her tape recorder. With a moan that was only half-feigned to cover the click, she pushed the On button.

Now they had Patrick.

That handy, high-powered tape machine was going to record a lot of inappropriate behavior in this elevator—moaning and sighing. Kissing noises, for sure. If she was lucky, words of lust and carnal intent. She intended to record the entire incident. No one could call it sexual harassment—she was an adult and at the moment couldn't be more consenting—but the tape would damage Saint Patrick, as her uncle derisively called him, and his credibility.

Naturally, she had no intention of actually having sex with Patrick—not to help her uncle achieve his revenge, anyway.

In fact, if it were anyone else who'd told her that Patrick had manufactured the lies that had cost her uncle—Councilor Cecil Thomson—the mayor's office, she wouldn't have believed him.

Her uncle had been Briana's biggest fan since her own parents were killed in a car accident when she was five.

She owed her upbringing, food, clothes and shelter to her mother's sister, Aunt Shirley, and her husband, Uncle Dennis; they'd given her a loving home and brought her up as their own.

But it was her mother's brother, Cecil, and his wife, Irene, who had financed her education, gymnastics instruction and piano lessons, even a couple of trips to Europe. And the extras that her legal guardians couldn't afford for her.

Her aunt and uncle back in Ohio had given her love and security when she was so lost and alone. From them she'd learned the values of hard work and frugality and the importance of honesty and loyalty. But Briana had had to share them with their own children.

Cecil and Irene had no children, so they always said Briana was like their own daughter. And there were times, she had to admit, when she'd cheerfully have changed her guardianship from the good, decent Dennis and Shirley to the charming and successful Cecil and Irene. Cecil was a big man with a bluff manner and a hearty laugh. He treated her like a princess and she adored him. She'd often wondered if she'd inherited her love of politics from him.

Briana had no interest in running for office, but the behind-the-scenes machinations of government fascinated her. And she'd discovered that small-scale government allowed her better scope for her talents. She could really make a difference. Cecil had guided her career, helping her attain the position of city manager in a small Midwest town.

Uncle Cecil had worked hard as a Courage Bay councilor for years. Of course, he had a full-time job as a banker, but she knew he got a lot more pleasure from politics than from banking. After the last mayor left office in disgrace, Uncle Cecil had discussed his plans with her to run for mayor himself and she'd eagerly offered to fly out and help with his campaign.

He'd chuckled. "Honey, I've lived in this town all my life. Managed the biggest local bank, served on council. There's nobody even running against me but a cocky young firefighter whose campaign donations couldn't fill his fireman's hat. When I'm mayor, I'll hire you as city manager."

But the call she'd received just a couple of weeks later hadn't been to tell her of his victory, but to warn her not to believe the lies that were being spread about him.

"That lying weasel fireman didn't have a hope. Not a goddamn hope of winning enough votes. So he and his cop buddies cooked up a story. I won't dirty your ears with hearing it, but let me tell you, the opposition's underhanded tactics have destroyed my chances. Worse, your aunt Irene was devastated." His voice had wavered as he told her the last part, and her heart went out to him. She knew how much he loved his wife.

Briana was furious. "How could anyone destroy a man's reputation and his marriage over a municipal election?" she'd cried, tears of rage almost choking her.

"They're lies, honey. All lies. I would never do...never do that to your aunt."

Of course, the minute she'd gotten off the phone with her uncle she'd started searching the Internet. It didn't take her long to access the electronic version of the *Courage Bay Sentinel*, the town's daily newspaper.

The paper had printed an old arrest photo of a man, supposedly her uncle, being booked for public lewdness. In fact, the twenty-year-old incident suggested her uncle had been caught having sex with a prostitute in a public place.

A man who would treat his niece with such love and generosity and who'd always had a close and loving relationship with his wife wouldn't do such a thing. Briana was sure of it, and if her uncle insisted the paper had printed lies, she believed him.

The next day, when she was calmer, she'd called him and suggested he sue the paper for libel and the police department for...well, she wasn't certain of the law, but there was obviously gross wrongdoing there, as well.

He'd heard her out, and then, in a voice that sounded old and defeated, said, "There's a record there, honey. It's false. I know it and you know it, but there's no way to prove that.

O'Shea—" he spat the word "—with his connections to the police, could easily pull this off. They've faked that photo and the arrest file, but it would be my word against theirs. I'll only hurt your aunt more by trying to fight their lies."

"But...but the prosti—the woman involved. Surely she'll testify on your behalf."

"She might, if she hadn't died more than five years ago. She was a drunk. Drove her car off the road." He laughed mirthlessly. "They set me up pretty good."

"This isn't right, Uncle Cecil. There must be something we can do to stop this injustice. Tell me. I'll do anything."

At the time, she'd had in mind letters to congress to initiate some kind of internal inquiry within the Courage Bay police department, getting the media involved, but her uncle stopped her. "I'll only make a fool of myself if I try to fight these boys. No. I'll never be mayor now." He sighed heavily and in that moment she knew how much becoming mayor had meant to him. "But revenge, they say, is a dish best served cold. Your support means the world to me, honey. I'll let you know when I need you."

And two months ago he'd done just that. Patrick O'Shea, the man who'd beaten her uncle by a landslide at the polls, needed a new administrative assistant. Her uncle was chuckling with glee at his perfect plan to arrange for the new mayor to be forced to resign for the same reasons as the former mayor. "As soon as he makes a pass at my beautiful niece, we've got him."

Although Briana was happy to do almost anything for her uncle, she wasn't at all keen on the idea of tempting a man sexually to destroy his political career. "I'm a feminist, Uncle Cecil. This sounds like something from the fifties."

"Darling girl, I'm not asking you to seduce him. If he's the moral saint he pretends to be, then nothing will happen. You'll do the job, I'll naturally make up the salary difference between your current salary and this one, and in, say, six months, if he hasn't acted inappropriately or made a pass at you, then we drop it."

Briana hadn't felt nearly as confident. But she did want to help her uncle, and she'd wanted to move to California, where she felt there were better employment opportunities, for a long time. "And if he does make a pass?"

"We'll have the tape to the media faster than you can say Monica Lewinsky."

"I've always pictured myself more as the Hillary Clinton type."

"Of course. You're bright and ambitious. You'll go places. But I know you're also deeply concerned about justice, and hate dirty politics. I'm offering you a chance to see justice done, and one ugly political wrong put right."

She bit her lip. She didn't like the plan. Didn't want to bring a man down. But she owed her uncle her loyalty. And he was right about her love of justice. Besides, if her new boss was an honorable man, he wouldn't make a pass at a female employee.

But if Patrick O'Shea was an honorable man, he never would have faked evidence against a decent, good person like her uncle. She'd do what her uncle asked in the name of justice and family loyalty, help clear up some civic corruption and then move on. With her work record, glowing letters of recommendation from former employers and an honors degree in government studies, she wouldn't have much trouble obtaining a challenging position, maybe in

Los Angeles or Sacramento. Reluctantly, she agreed to Uncle Cecil's plan.

Briana hadn't been thrilled about the part she was to play before she arrived in Courage Bay and interviewed for the job, but she was even less happy when she met Patrick O'Shea and felt her mouth go dry.

The man was gorgeous in an understated, rugged, pick-a-woman-up-and-carry-her-across-a-raging-river kind of way. He had black hair with a few silver strands beginning to show, and Irish blue eyes that could twinkle with amusement or turn a hard, cold pewter when there was trouble. When he gazed at her, his eyes darkened in intensity. He might not say anything, but she knew what he was thinking. She didn't think seducing him would be much of a trial.

Men came on to her all the time. It was something she'd been used to since she was a teenager. With her Nordic genes and statuesque body, she was accustomed to male attention. However, it was unusual for her to respond as forcefully as she did to Patrick O'Shea. She was only sorry that someone she found so attractive should be so corrupt.

Of course, whatever his standards, she considered herself a woman of integrity. She wouldn't make the first move. It was up to him. But her tape recorder was always in her purse and the batteries fresh.

She'd discovered in the first week of working for the mayor that when he was out of the office, he sometimes made notes into a small personal recorder. Periodically, he'd give her the recorder and ask her to transcribe his notes, which ranged from budget issues to ideas for future speeches.

The recorder was common enough, and by the second

week of her employment, she owned an identical one. She reasoned that if Patrick ever caught sight of hers, he'd naturally think it was his own. Not that she intended for him to notice she had a tape recorder, but she believed in covering all her bases.

In two months, nothing had happened.

Nothing that you could put on tape, anyway. Things like sizzling eye contact. A sudden rise in air temperature that had nothing to do with a faulty air conditioner. And a longing deep inside her that was as rare as it was potent.

Briana had never found herself in a worse predicament. She wanted Patrick O'Shea. She wanted to run her fingers over the rugged planes of his face, trace the shape of his ears, the scar that bisected one eyebrow.

Even though his next birthday would be his fortieth, he still had the lean hard body of an active firefighter. She knew he trained frequently at the gym with the guys from his former station.

She wanted to touch that powerfully built body. She had fantasies of coming together with him naked. Fantasies that shamed her because he was her boss and it was inappropriate for her to think about having sex with him.

The curse of her situation was that if he did make a pass, she'd know he was as hot for her as she was for him.

And if he made a pass, she'd also know that he was a hypocrite. A man who would make sexual overtures to a female employee after promising to act with squeaky clean ethics was beneath contempt.

But now here they were, in this dark elevator, and it was Briana's body, not her brain, that was in charge. Still thrumming with adrenaline after their brush with death, she suddenly didn't care much about ethics or campaign promises.

As his lips crushed hers, Briana responded helplessly, even as she wished deep down that Patrick had turned out to be a better man.

Five minutes. She'd give him five minutes. Enough time to get some moaning and groaning recorded. If he was like every other man she'd ever kissed, he'd try to get her out of her clothes.

She'd say no.

He'd beg her for sex.

And she'd have him. On tape.

The man is a hypocrite and a liar, she reminded herself as Patrick's lips found her throat and she tipped her chin to give him better access.

Five minutes. She traced the shape of his eyebrow, noting the indent of his scar, then let her hands roam his face, his shoulders. His arousal strained against her, hard, seeking her softest parts, and she couldn't stop the rush of longing.

Stuck there in the dark, suspended between floors was like being caught between reality and fantasy.

Patrick O'Shea was a bad man.

She knew it. He'd destroyed her uncle's chances of ever becoming mayor of the town he'd served for a quarter of a century. Now, the minute they were stuck in an elevator together, he was jumping her bones. Intellectually, she knew he was a hypocrite and a liar. But the trouble was, her body didn't care. Her flesh and blood responded to him in a purely physical sense that had nothing to do with morals or ethics, elections or earthquakes.

Well, earthquakes maybe, in their crudest "the earth moved" definition.

"I want you so much," he murmured against her neck.

Damn. Too soft for the tape recorder.

Her breathing shallow, she raised her head and spoke as clearly as she could. "What did you say?"

"I want you so much, Briana," he repeated. "I want to make love with you."

"Yes," she said, not certain whether she meant yes as in *Yes! I got it on tape,* or *Yes! He wants me, he wants me.*

Patrick seemed to take it as *Yes, she wants me.* He went back to kissing her neck, which was fine, because she did want him. More than she ever remembered wanting anything.

He made it to the base of her throat, and she found herself arching up to give him easier access to her breasts.

His hands, so capable and strong, cupped her breasts with hot abandon, surprising a moan out of her.

As though impatient to reach bare skin—and he couldn't be more impatient for it than she was—he plunged a hand into the vee of her blouse, then cursed in frustration.

"Buttons," she cried, desperate to feel his hands on her. She'd have undone them herself, but her arms were supporting her and they trembled beneath her.

He made such clumsy work of her buttons that Briana realized he was shaking as badly as she was.

The tape, she recalled dimly. It would be impossible to register what he was doing on tape.

"Are you taking off my blouse?"

A low chuckle answered her. "I'm trying, but damn it, I'm out of practice."

That blunt admission gave her pause. Of course, she

knew he'd been a widower for three years, but surely… He was a man. He must have…

Anyway, none of that mattered. What mattered was getting him to incriminate himself on tape so she could do her buttons back up and be done with this unpleasant task of entrapping a man she'd grown to like.

Even if her judgment was suspect, she did like him. She wanted to get this over with. Record the incident. Get out of here alive. Give the tape to her uncle and leave town.

Playing this devious undercover game was no fun. She'd discovered within hours of meeting Patrick that she wasn't cut out for entrapment. She liked plain dealing and honesty. He might be a lying, devious career-destroyer, but at this moment, so was she, no matter how she tried to justify her actions.

Mentally, she reviewed the tape. There'd be kissing sounds, heavy breathing, Patrick admitting he wanted her…

That would have to be enough. She couldn't do this anymore.

She opened her mouth to stop him but at the same moment he managed to unsnap her bra. In the dark, her nipples tightened, then she gasped as his hot tongue slid across her aching flesh.

"Oh," she cried, her entire body shuddering. "That feels *so* good."

His tongue curled around one nipple and he sucked the tip of her breast right into his mouth. He was so greedy, so eager, and his obvious delight in her thrilled her more than any refined technique.

From one breast to the other he moved eagerly, as

though he'd been in prison for years and had only now rediscovered women.

He was panting, she was panting. The tape must be moving into R-rated territory.

His hand was working its way under her skirt. She was supposed to stop him, she had to say…

"No."

The word was a piteous groan, and Briana realized it hadn't come from her.

"God, Briana, I'm sorry." It was Patrick who'd spoken.

"No?" She felt stunned, rejected. "What do you mean, no?"

He stroked her hair, touched her cheek.

"I want to make love to you right now, more than I've ever wanted anything. But—"

"No buts." Her body burned for him, her flesh felt as though steam must be rising from it. They'd obviously denied the powerful attraction of each other's pheromones for too long.

She kissed him, hard and deep, teasing his lips with her tongue, the sensations so much stronger in the dark.

"But I—"

A finger across his lips silenced him. "I believe in fate," she told him. "Fate stuck us in this elevator and turned out the lights. What happens tomorrow doesn't matter. Hell, Patrick, we almost didn't have a tomorrow."

"I know, but—"

"I don't want to think about how long we're going to be trapped here. I don't want to think about how awful it would be to develop claustrophobia in the next ten minutes. The best way to fight boredom and fear is to occupy your mind."

"You think?" Reluctant humor threaded his tone.

"I know." She smiled in the dark, smug, knowing she'd won.

"I… You're still a female employee."

She loosened his tie. "So fire me."

That surprised laughter out of him. She felt it rumble up his throat beneath her fingers. "Fire you? You're phenomenal. Competent, smart, hardworking. Hell, why would I fire you?"

"So we can have sex. It's temporary. You can rehire me whenever we get out of here."

There was a long pause, and she could almost hear him thinking. She held her breath. She hadn't been entirely joking about needing to take her mind off their current situation.

She wasn't claustrophobic, but she knew that Patrick was keeping her thoughts and feelings more pleasantly engaged. As it was, the reality of being trapped in a warm black box tickled the edges of her mind. And that box was hanging from a cable that had sustained a major earthquake and some hefty aftershocks in the past month. Who knew how long it would hold?

No. She needed a distraction. And sex with Patrick was about the best damn distraction she could imagine.

"Briana?"

"Yes?"

"You're fired."

A great rush of pent-up breath left her chest, and the next second she wished she'd saved a little, for Patrick was kissing the life out of her.

Somehow she was on her back, the elevator tile hard beneath her spine, but as for the rest of her…oh my. Now that Patrick had let himself go, he was all over her.

He kissed her hungrily while his hands roamed everywhere. She heard a small tear and then the bounce of a plastic button on the tile.

"Sorry," he said, his voice so husky with passion she barely recognized it.

"It's okay," she murmured, loving his eagerness, finding the clumsiness endearing. He was so gorgeous and confident it hadn't occurred to her that his technique would be less than smooth.

Then his mouth found her breast again and she put all rational thought away.

"Oh, yes." Her body arched beneath him.

His hand was warm, slightly leathery as it slid beneath her skirt and trailed up, up to where she was so very hot.

Even as he cupped her through her panties, she felt everything tighten, all those wonderfully concentrated sensation centers started tuning up ready to sing.

Her blouse was open, her bra gaping, but he was still dressed. She attacked his buttons with barely more finesse than he'd shown. She wanted to feel his naked skin against hers. Wanted the warm roughness against her sensitive skin.

She got the buttons out of the way and parted his shirt, running her hands over the strong muscular planes of his stomach, the bulge of his pecs, lightly fuzzed with hair.

She pulled him to her, rubbing against him like a cat against a favorite couch. He was fuzzy, warm, strong and so very alive.

His fingers slipped inside her panties and she jerked her hips up against him, begging wordlessly and shamelessly to be touched.

As his fingers played over her, she began to sigh, her breath coming in panting gasps.

"I want you inside me," she cried.

His fingers slowed and he kissed her softly. "I don't have anything with me."

"Hmm?" she murmured, feeling slightly muzzy.

"Protection. Condoms. I don't—"

"Oh. Right." She was on the pill, but still, a condom was sensible. That's why she always carried a few. "I think I have some in my purse." Once again she dug around in her bag.

Briana wasn't a promiscuous woman, but she believed in being prepared. She had a discreet little zip-up bag in blue Chinese silk in there somewhere.

Trouble was, a woman as prepared as she was tended to have a lot of other junk filling her bag, as well. Cell phone…she paused with her hand on it. She could at least try to phone out, maybe get them rescued sooner. But then she'd miss her chance to make love with Patrick, and right now her body's urges were overpowering her common sense ten to one.

She dug deeper, fingertips searching for the touch of silk. She felt the tape recorder. Once again her hand stilled. Oh, lord. She'd forgotten all about the tape. She bit her lip in the dark. She should turn it off. After all, Patrick had fired her temporarily so they could avoid any hint of scandal.

But…

She'd think about that later. She could always erase the tape.

She kept digging, feeling Patrick's breath on her belly, his hands roving with growing confidence, warm and sure as they drove her slowly, but inevitably higher.

He put his mouth on her nipple and she drew in a sharp breath. Longing rippled through her. She couldn't hang on much longer.

Silk. Purse. There it was, right at the bottom. She pulled it out, along with a travel pack of tissues, and handed it to him.

She heard the zip as he opened the silk pouch. Then she heard the rustle of plastic tearing.

"What the—"

"What is it?" Briana asked.

"I know I'm out of practice, but have condoms changed?" He sounded not only puzzled but mildly grossed out.

"What are you—"

He shoved the small package in her hand and she felt inside. At first she registered only confusion as her fingers touched something soft, wet and cold. Then the spring-fresh scent hit her and she giggled. "That's not a condom. It's a travel wipe."

A pause. Even in the dark she felt him staring at her.

"You're kidding me."

She stifled another giggle. He sounded amazed and put out at the same time. "I keep them in the same bag. I like to be prepared."

"You got cigarettes and brandy in there for afterward?"

"You'll have to wait and see," she teased, digging in to the silk pouch and identifying a packet that definitely contained a condom. "Here."

This time the ripping sound was much slower, and she could tell he was examining the condom before withdrawing it from its package.

He must have been satisfied, for she felt a movement beside her that suggested he was putting it on.

It was so dark, and he felt so good, she wouldn't think about tomorrow—or even tonight, after they were rescued.

There was only now. Her body yearned for him, open and wanting, their isolation only increasing the sense of intimacy and mystery.

Because there was no light, she learned his body by touch, as he learned hers.

Darkness, she discovered, was a potent aphrodisiac.

CHAPTER THREE

PATRICK KNEW that as long as he lived, he'd never forget this night.

The dream that had haunted him for two months since Briana walked into his office was turning into a reality. She was so warm and soft, womanly and exciting, so exactly as he'd imagined.

She smelled like fresh rain, felt like soft velvet, and her skin tasted like warm, willing woman. With a rush of potent longing he wanted to taste all of her. But right at this moment he needed to bury himself deep inside her body more than he needed to breathe.

And she was begging him to do exactly that.

"Please…" Her voice was trembling with excitement. "Come inside me. I can't wait any longer."

"Whatever the lady wants," he said softly, settling between her thighs.

He kissed her deeply. He wanted her to know what this meant to him, what she meant to him.

"Briana, I—"

"Now, *please.*" She grasped his shaft and placed him at the hot slick entrance to her body.

Raw need took hold of him and he thrust hard and deep into heaven.

Her wordless cry of pleasure filled his ears, her warmth surrounded him, her scent delighted him as he thrust, wishing he could prolong this sensual buildup forever, knowing he'd be done in an embarrassingly short time.

It had been so long.

As her body arched to meet him, as she thrashed mindlessly against him, he slipped a hand between their bodies and touched her. The timbre of her cries changed, becoming deeper, more guttural. Knowing she was close, he let himself go a little more, riding her hard, loving the way she hooked her legs around him and stayed with him all the way.

He felt the moment she surrendered, felt her body clench around his shaft, and he lost his own control, feeling the surge of powerful pleasure as he emptied himself into her.

Then he collapsed, damp and spent against her, and she wrapped her arms around him and stroked his hair.

Finally, he thought dimly, after two months of torment. Finally.

He kissed her softly, thinking he'd never ride this elevator again without remembering….

Along with an awkwardness that his knees felt bruised from rubbing on the hard floor of the elevator came a reminder of his responsibilities. His first thought was for his kids. Had they been scared? He wished he'd been there when the ground started to shake. At least he had a reliable housekeeper. Then he turned his mind to the emergency crews. What was going on in his city while he was stuck in this dangling box?

PATRICK GLANCED at his watch. Even in the dark, Briana knew what he was doing. She could see the pale green numbers glowing in the dark. Did he want to be rid of her already?

An hour or so ago, when they'd rebuttoned themselves, he'd tried the emergency phone installed in the elevator, but it wasn't working. He'd cursed, frustration coming off him in waves, and she'd thought to herself, *Wham, bam, thank you, ma'am.*

Since then, they'd sat side by side on the hard floor. He'd become fidgety and morose. He checked his watch again. She felt his impatience, heard it echo around in the dark elevator as his feet tapped the floor.

"What time is it?" she asked.

"Hmm?" For the third time he turned his wrist to stare at his watch.

"Ten-fifteen." His breath exploded out of him. "The baby-sitter is expecting me home. What's she going to do when I don't show up?"

Since that was obviously a rhetorical question, she didn't answer directly. Instead, she reached out, touching his arm in a comforting gesture.

He wasn't acting this way because he wanted to be rid of her now they'd had sex. Patrick was a single dad. A fact that she'd allowed herself to forget. He had responsibilities, children who needed him home.

She hung her head, knowing he couldn't see her guilty face in the dark. Inside her bag was her cell phone—a fact she hadn't bothered sharing with him because she'd been so busy trying to lure him into indiscretion.

She had a choice.

She could continue to pretend there was no phone in her bag.

Or she could admit to the phone, hoping her acting abilities were good enough that he'd believe she'd forgotten the stupid thing or simply assumed it wouldn't work.

A long, silent minute ensued. She felt his urgency and her own conflicted feelings.

But most of all, she found herself remembering how it felt to be parentless. That sense of utter desolation—that you didn't belong to anyone anymore. That the place where you were safest and most special was gone forever, along with those who'd loved you best.

Patrick's son, Dylan, was nine, little Fiona five. She'd met them a couple of times at the office and she'd liked them. They were quiet, well-behaved kids. Both times they'd come with their Aunt Shannon, Patrick's firefighter sister, and the four of them had gone out for lunch. She could see that lunch with Dad was a big treat.

They must have been so young when their mother died.

She took a deep breath. He was never going to believe she'd forgotten she had her phone. She'd have to go with the brainless angle, which irked her.

"Is there a chance my cell phone would work?" she asked simply.

The silence thickened. "You have a cell phone on you?"

"In my bag. Yes."

"Why didn't you say so earlier?"

Because I wanted you to seduce me so I could ruin your political career. She couldn't say that, so she stuck with dumb. "But surely all the phone lines will be affected by the aftershock."

"Briana, cell phones work by satellite. It might not work in an elevator, but let's give it a try."

She dug into her bag, pulled out her cell and handed it to him.

She felt his haste and then saw the eerie green glow as he flipped open the phone.

As he punched numbers and the call went through, she felt more and more like an evil woman keeping a single father from the children who needed him.

"Mrs. Simpson? It's Patrick. How's everyone? Are the kids safe? Did the earthquake scare them?"

He must have liked the answers he was getting because she felt him relax, and his tone became less urgent.

"Look, I'm going to be late. I'm stuck in an elevator at work. That's right. No. I'm fine. Can you stay? It could be morning before we get out of here. Depends what the damage is like."

She heard him give a sigh of relief. "Are Fiona and Dylan asleep? Good. Please go ahead and sleep in the guest room. I'm sorry about this. Right. I'll see you then."

He hung up and blew out a long breath. "The babysitter can stay," he said, handing her back the phone. "Thank God everyone's all right."

Then he sank back against the elevator wall.

She chuckled. She couldn't stop herself.

"What's funny?"

"I'm thinking, since the cell phone works, maybe we should make a second call. Like to 911, to get us out of here."

He laughed right along with her, a deep, rich sound, as though she'd made the funniest joke he'd ever heard. "Sorry, I got so caught up in my kids I wasn't thinking straight." And that, she thought, ought to let her off the hook for not telling him about her cell phone earlier. After an earthquake, not thinking straight seemed a perfectly acceptable excuse. For a lot of things.

Thank goodness it was dark, so Patrick couldn't see her smile. Once he knew his kids were fine, he was obviously so happy to stay stuck here with her that it didn't matter to him when they were rescued. Truth was, she was just as happy.

Right now, her body still pulsing with its own aftershocks of remembered pleasure, she could simply enjoy her new lover's closeness, reach out and touch him if she liked, lean into him and inhale the all male scent of his skin.

She heard Patrick's voice on the phone to the 911 operator. He called her by name. Dorothy. Of course, he probably knew all the 911 operators from his days as fire chief. Whatever he'd done to get the job, he was a good mayor. He asked about the damage elsewhere in the city.

She heard his tone change, and he uttered a sharp-edged curse.

"No, Dorothy," he said. "We're fine. Put us on lowest priority. I don't care. I want the full crew on that basement suite fire. Any idea how many people are inside?"

Briana's warm and fuzzy postcoital glow faded fast. She'd been so caught up with her own predicament, she hadn't considered that there were other people in town who hadn't fared as well as she had.

"What else is going on, Dorothy? Come on. No BS. I need to know."

She didn't even think, but reached out to grab his free hand, knowing he was hearing bad news and was powerless to do anything to help.

"Oh, no," he said. "I take my kids to that corner store

for Saturday afternoon treats after Dylan's baseball games. Is the fatality confirmed?"

He sighed deeply and she knew the answer. "Just the one?"

Here she and Patrick had been celebrating their own escape from disaster, and someone had been killed.

"No...just a minute." He turned to Briana. "There are some fires and a collapsed building in town. Okay with you if we go to the bottom of the list? We'll be rescued by morning, but I'm not sure exactly when."

Well, her bladder would start complaining at some point, and she could use a meal, but she wasn't all that uncomfortable, and it was tough to ask for priority treatment when people were in a lot more desperate straits than she was. So Briana squeezed his hand as a thank-you for asking. "Of course, I'm fine."

He squeezed back. "You're one in a million," he said, then turned back to the phone. "We're fine, Dorothy. I'll give you the cell phone number here. We'll call again if anything changes, but so far we're stable."

He ended the call and handed Briana her phone. She felt as though a huge weight had been lifted off her chest. Even if she'd owned up to her phone earlier, nothing would have changed. She knew Patrick would have made the same decision then that he'd made now. The people of Courage Bay came first.

She sighed, and leaned into him. "How bad is it?"

"One confirmed fatality. The convenience store near my house collapsed tonight. A woman died when a falling beam hit her. She's unidentified so far. Probably the cashier."

She touched his shoulder in comfort. If the convenience

store was near his home, chances were that Patrick knew the woman.

"And you said something about a fire?"

"Yes. House fire. Looks to be contained in a basement suite over on Eighth. The fire crew's still working on it. No idea yet if there was anyone inside." He cursed, softly and viciously. "If council hadn't vetoed my motions to add to the emergency forces, maybe we could have responded quicker."

Briana swallowed an unpleasant lump in her throat. She knew as well as anyone that it was her uncle Cecil who was leading the pack that kept vetoing Patrick's proposals. Uncle Cecil referred to the new mayor as a hothead, and Patrick was just young enough, and passionate enough, that the notion took with the primarily older, established members of council. They had voted with her uncle against Patrick.

"None of the councilors have ever gone through anything like this before," she said hesitantly, instinctively defending her uncle's actions, even though Patrick had no notion of her close relationship to his bitter enemy.

"Well, it's time they dragged their heads out of their asses and took a look around. People have died needlessly because we couldn't respond effectively when they needed help."

She noticed he said "we" when he referred to the rescue teams, and Briana realized that even though he was mayor now, Patrick still identified with the emergency personnel.

Following her train of thought, she asked, "Why did you give up being fire chief to go for the mayor's job?" Even to her own ears, she sounded wistful. For a moment she daydreamed that he hadn't ever done such a thing. Then her uncle would be mayor and she would undoubtedly have come to Courage Bay for a visit, or to work for Uncle Cecil, as he'd planned.

In a city of eighty-five thousand, she might easily have met Patrick O'Shea the fire chief, and how different everything would have been. She was single; he was single. There would have been no reason for them to deny the instant and powerful attraction that had sprung up between them.

"I was mad as hell," he said. "The former mayor made a joke out of our town. I got on my high horse and told anyone who wanted to listen my ideas for how to improve Courage Bay."

He laughed softly. "Some of my friends got together and raised a few bucks for a campaign and put my name forward. I was already a declared candidate before I'd even made up my mind."

"Do you miss being a firefighter?" she asked.

"I miss the action. I miss being able to do something right now that's going to save a life. I'd rather face a twenty-foot wall of fire than some of the council meetings I've been stuck in lately. But I've got kids and…"

He didn't finish the sentence, but she immediately guessed the real reason behind the switch. Once his wife had died, he didn't want to continue in a dangerous job and risk orphaning his kids. Good for him.

"How about you?" he asked her. "You know as well as I do that you're overqualified for this job. In fact, you almost didn't get it because of that fact."

"Really? Who wanted to pass on me, you or Archie?" Archie Weld, the communications manager for the city, had interviewed her first. Only the final candidates had gone on to interviews with Patrick.

"Don't hit me, but I was the one with concerns."

Smart guy.

"Archie talked me into hiring you. He said the way things were going in our city this past year with the mudslides, the fires, the earthquakes and murders that I'd be crazy not to jump on you." He cleared his throat and said, with a touch of humor, "Figuratively speaking of course."

"Of course."

"I assumed you were taking the job to get a foot in the door, and then you'd start applying for more challenging positions. But I was wrong, wasn't I? I still can't figure out why you took the job."

She was on shaky ground, but she wanted to be as honest as she could with the man she'd just made love with. "I wanted a change from the Midwest. I've always loved California. So, you're right in one way. But I won't start looking for another job right away. That wouldn't be fair to you."

"I don't want to argue with you, but based on what—"

"Then don't argue," she said, cutting him off with a kiss. It took her a few times to find his mouth. First she kissed his cheek, the bump of his nose and finally his lips. When she finally pulled back, she said, "Looks like we're stuck here for a while longer." Her voice dropped to a sexy whisper. "Just the two of us, in the dark." She ran her index finger up his arm. "I can think of one way to help pass the time."

Even as she tipped her head toward him, his hand was cradling the back of her head and his lips covered hers. Give the man credit, he wasn't slow on the uptake.

"PATRICK? BRIANA? You okay?" The strong clear female voice jerked Briana awake. She heard the welcome whirr of the generator and then the sound of thumping and banging.

As she lifted her head from Patrick's shoulder, which she'd used as a pillow, a sharp crick in her neck had her stifling a howl of pain. She rubbed her neck while Patrick squeezed her shoulder, then rose to his feet and moved toward the front of the elevator.

"Hey, Shannon!" he yelled. "Hope we didn't haul you out of bed for this."

"For that crack, you get to buy the coffee."

"Get us out of here and I'll buy you breakfast. Anything you want." He turned to Briana. "My sister, Shannon," he said, overly cheerful. "She's a truckie on Engine One. She's the best."

"Great," Briana said, equally hearty as she struggled to her feet.

Already the real world was close and awkwardness crowded in as they stood together listening to the noises indicating imminent rescue.

Suddenly Patrick pulled her to him and kissed her hot and hard.

He took her hands and held them loosely. She wished she could see his face, but even though the generator was thrumming, the elevator was still in darkness. "I'm going to have to give you your job back now. Are you sure you want it?"

Silence pressed against her chest. She understood what he was saying. The minute she accepted her job back, the affair ended.

She could leave the mayor's staff now that she had the tape, of course. But after tonight, she knew she'd never use it. No. What had happened between them had been as unexpected and bizarre as the aftershock that had trapped them in the elevator.

There'd been a lot of time in the night to think. She'd intended to tape Patrick making an inappropriate pass. She would say no, loud and clear, then record him trying to talk her into having sex. The reality was pretty much the opposite. Patrick had tried to say no and Briana had thrown herself at him. She knew her uncle believed Patrick had faked the evidence that destroyed Cecil's chances of ever becoming mayor. She'd believed it, too. Who else had anything to gain by publishing a doctored picture and leaking a bogus story? Now, however, she was beginning to wonder if Patrick actually had anything to do with leaking false evidence against his rival Maybe someone on his campaign team had done the deed. Possibly, they hadn't even told him.

Okay, it was a slim chance, but she'd just made love with the man. She wanted him to be as decent as he'd seemed in the two months she'd worked for him.

One way or another, she'd find out who had blackened her uncle's name. If that person was Patrick, then she'd do what she had to do.

She owed her uncle her loyalty.

But after tonight, she felt she owed Patrick some, too.

"I can't stay fired," she told him with real regret. "You need me."

He touched her face, and she felt tenderness in his fingertips. "You have no idea how much," he said.

CHAPTER FOUR

THE SOUNDS OF their approaching rescuers had Briana and Patrick pulling reluctantly apart.

"Okay, guys, stand back now," Shannon's voice came through the metal door, and before Briana could take a step backward, Patrick was reaching for her hand. Not that she was scared anymore, but it was nice to have the comfort of his warm hand in hers. A loud bang sounded, then a creak, followed by the screech of metal pulling against metal.

As light flooded the elevator, Briana freed her hand from Patrick's and shaded her eyes.

"Good to see you, kid," Patrick said to his sister. Anyone could tell they were related, Briana thought every time she saw the siblings together. Both were tall, athletic, black-haired and blue-eyed. They shared the trademark O'Shea grin she'd also seen in his children.

The grin on both faces was particularly broad this time. Briana knew that not all Shannon's rescues turned out this well, yet she risked her life day after day, as her brother had done in his previous career.

In full uniform, Shannon seemed tough, and she was, but Briana knew she had a soft heart under all the protective gear.

The elevator had come to a stop about three feet above the main floor, so they had to bend down and jump to get out. Patrick naturally gestured for Briana to go first. She did, pulling off her high-heeled shoes and clutching the hands of Shannon and another firefighter. She managed to land on her feet without any injury, other than to her pride.

"I think you lost a button in there," Shannon said in an undertone just after Briana landed.

A quick glance down showed her blouse gaping open to display a good bit of cleavage and the ice-blue silk of her bra. Briana grabbed the front of her blouse to cover the gap, forcing back the blush that threatened. It didn't help that she caught one of the male firefighters checking her out with an interested expression on his face. She gave him the ice-queen don't-even-think-about-it look she'd perfected in high school and turned back to Patrick's sister.

"It must have come off when the elevator lurched and threw us to the ground," she said.

"Must have," Shannon replied in a dry tone, giving Briana a look that suggested more than her button was missing.

Briana knew she must appear mussed and hastily put back together. She detected the same telltale pewter color in Shannon's eyes that were a dead giveaway in Patrick's that he was angry about something. In this case, Briana realized that Shannon had made an educated guess at what had happened in that dark elevator and she didn't like it one bit.

Patrick landed beside Briana a moment later and she couldn't stop herself from looking up at him, seeing him in the light for the first time since they'd made love.

The blush she'd managed to suppress a minute ago swept over her cheeks now as she read the passion, intimacy and some other emotion she didn't want to name deep in Patrick's eyes. His weren't pewter now, but the deepest Irish-Sea-on-a-sunny-day blue she'd ever seen them.

Her heart seemed to stutter as the full impact of what she'd done hit.

"Patrick, I—"

"You forgot your purse," Shannon said, reaching up into the elevator to haul Briana's bag off the floor and hand it to her.

"Thanks," Briana said shortly, grabbing the thing. Her bag hid so much. The evidence of their passion, tucked neatly away, and that tape recorder, which she'd managed to switch off before their second bout of lovemaking.

"Well, I guess you missed your meeting with the police chief," she said to Patrick.

"Yes." He grimaced. "I doubt he even noticed. I bet he's had a busier night than I did."

She stared at him, and he must have realized what he'd said, for it was his turn to display ruddy cheeks. She and Patrick had not been idle in that elevator.

They were saved from awkwardness by the second firefighter, who said, "It's been a busy night for EMS all right. Another one."

It was no longer night but morning now, Briana realized. Almost 3:00 a.m. If she weren't torn between elation and guilt over what had transpired in that elevator, she'd probably be pretty tired.

"What's happening out there?" Patrick asked his sister, reverting from the tender loving man of the past few hours to the mayor of a town once again facing disaster.

"Not good," Shannon told him, her voice neutral. It was

a tone Briana had come to associate with emergency personnel who were sometimes forced to give the worst news possible. "One woman was killed in the convenience store collapse. She'd been pinned under a beam, and by the time we got there..." She shook her head. "There was a second woman, a fire victim. We pulled her out of the basement suite still alive, but I wouldn't put her chances of recovery past fair."

Shannon's emotionless delivery almost fooled Briana into thinking Shannon was taking the violent deaths in her stride, but not her brother.

"Hey, kid. I'm sorry," he said, pulling his sister in for a hug, regardless of her bulky uniform and helmet.

Amazingly, the tough, strong woman of a second ago let herself lean on her older brother. "Yeah," she said, and in that one word Briana heard fatigue, despair and anger. "If we weren't so stretched, and all of us running on too little sleep, maybe we could have got there sooner. Maybe—"

"You can't beat yourself up over this. You know that. Sometimes there are fatalities." Patrick spoke with the authority of a former firefighter who'd been there and seen it all, but he still held his sister in his arms.

Shannon couldn't see his face, but Briana could, and almost as though she'd read his mind, she knew he was doing exactly what he'd told Shannon not to do. Blaming himself for the stretched resources, the exhausted emergency crews—the deaths of two more Courage Bay's citizens.

Their brief romantic idyll, Briana realized, was over.

"I'm going to go home and get some sleep," she announced. "I'll see you at the office tomorrow."

"Wait," Patrick said. "Let me drive you home."

She smiled at him, wishing it were that easy. Wishing she could just say yes. "No. My car's in the lot. You get home and check on your kids. I'll see you in the morning."

"Are you sure?" The words were urgent, the meaning behind them obvious to Briana, but, she hoped, not to the other ears listening in. He was asking if she really wanted to keep working for him. Since her other choice was sleeping with him, it was one of the hardest things she'd ever done when she said, "Yes. I'm sure."

He nodded reluctantly. "Sleep in tomorrow morning." He shook his head. "I guess I mean *this* morning. Come in to work when you can. I'd give you the whole day off, but frankly, I'm going to need all the help I can get."

Briana knew that the phone was going to be ringing like crazy tomorrow as city residents phoned in to complain about the latest disaster and the city's response.

The media would hound Patrick; councilors would be calling, as would the fire chief and the police chief. On top of that, she had a pretty good notion that once the story spread that he'd been trapped in the elevator, his family and friends would be on the hotline making sure he was okay. It was going to be a busy day. As kind as it was of her boss to offer her the morning off, Briana knew she wouldn't take him up on it.

He needed her.

As soon as she'd given her car a quick check, Briana drove carefully through the quiet streets. She went more slowly than usual, since a couple of the traffic lights were out, probably due to the aftershock. Maybe it was a result of being cooped up in that dark elevator so long, but the first thing she'd done when she started the engine was to roll down all the windows. She decided to take the route that hugged the coastline on the outskirts of the city, and as she drove, she could hear the quiet shush of the ocean, smell the clean air coming off the bay. She tried not to think too much about what had happened to her personally tonight.

She'd vowed not to sleep with the man she was trying to topple, so how had she come to do it?

It was easy to blame circumstances. The euphoria following their escape from serious injury or death. The intimacy of being together for all those hours. Briana knew she could have managed to get through a hurtling fall in an elevator and a few hours in the dark with any other man and not jump his bones. But Patrick O'Shea was not most men. And the plain truth was, their attraction had been immediate and intense from the first moment they'd met.

As she drove home, she tried to convince herself that nothing monumental had happened. That it was only sex. And that everything would go back to the way it had been before the aftershock.

When she finally reached the apartment she rented on the main floor of a house, she was still keyed up. Her eyes were gritty with fatigue, but she knew she wouldn't be able to sleep for a while.

Besides, her stomach reminded her that she'd missed dinner. Unable to face cooking, she toasted whole-wheat bread, dished up a bowl of yogurt and sliced a banana into it. She poured a glass of apple cider to accompany "dinner." While she ate, she flipped through the day's mail. A couple of bills, a promotional flyer from a high-end fashion store and this month's copy of *Gourmet*

Magazine, which she subscribed to, even though she barely had time to cook for herself these days, never mind entertain.

Still, there was something about reading up on other people's elegant dinner parties, checking out the international destinations featured, and imagining she was tasting all those wonderfully photographed dishes that made up in a small way for the fact that too many of her meals lately had been like this one.

She had dinner tidied away by 4:00 a.m. and was no more tired than she had been earlier. So she drew a hot bath, throwing a few handfuls of lavender milk crystals under the running faucet. While the tub was filling, she fetched a clean nightgown and her slippers.

When at last she eased herself into the warm, silky milk bath, magazine at hand, Briana breathed deeply of the lavender, in dire need of its soothing aromatherapy benefits.

She was in the middle of reading about a romantic springtime feast for two, when she caught herself changing places with the attractive couple in the magazine. She projected Patrick into the photo with her, fantasizing about him sitting across the cozy round table, toasting her with the California sauvignon blanc, eating the food she'd cooked and staring warmly into her eyes.

Smiling slightly to herself, she went back over their evening. Her spine was a little sore in places, and there was definitely some incipient whisker burn on the slope of one breast. She touched the spot. Next time, they'd have to find a bed.

Next time…

She got out of the bath with more haste than grace, slopping water on her magazine in her agitation. What the hell was she doing? Patrick was a good man. She was sure of it.

Drying off and pulling on her robe, she reminded herself that Uncle Cecil was a good man, too. But Patrick couldn't have deliberately damaged her uncle's career and her aunt's peace of mind. There had to be another explanation.

Someone had done it, though, and Briana was going to find out who.

She washed her face, brushed her teeth and crawled into bed, knowing she'd be crawling out again in three hours. She only hoped she could manage to sleep some of the time.

Tomorrow was going to be a very busy day.

PATRICK STAYED at city hall long enough to make sure the fire department had put up emergency tape over the elevator doors.

"Thanks for getting us out of there," Patrick had said to the crew as they left. Since he knew them all, he hadn't bothered with the formality of handshakes, but slapped them on the back and joked around a little. Shannon had hung back and made sure she had a minute alone with her brother.

"You okay?" she'd asked.

"Sure. I don't think I even got bruised when the elevator jolted."

"Don't play dumb with me, big bro. You know what I'm talking about. You and your model-gorgeous secretary looked like you were rolling out of bed when you got out of the elevator."

"So we fell asleep while we were waiting. Get your nose out of my business."

Whatever she'd guessed had gone on in that elevator, it was only a guess. He didn't feel like talking about what had really happened, why and what he felt about it, because he wasn't even sure himself.

Like most of his family, Shannon had urged him to get back out and start dating again. But he didn't think sex in the elevator with his admin assistant was quite what she'd had in mind.

It wasn't what he'd had in mind, either. But he had a feeling fate had taken a hand in his love life. And he was feeling pretty damned grateful to fate.

"I'm fine," he said to his sister, and she knew him well enough to know that if he didn't feel like saying more, he wouldn't.

"You don't look fine. You look like an eager boy with his first crush."

"I can handle it." He grinned ruefully. "At least I think I can. Speaking of nosy questions about love, how's John?"

Shannon's tired eyes brightened at the mention of John Forester, the man she'd fallen for last summer. He was still living in New York and they were making do with a long-distance relationship. She sighed. "He asked me to move in with him."

"In New York?"

She nodded. "Don't say anything to anyone else. I don't know what I'm going to do yet."

"Can't he be a modern man and move out here where all your family and friends are?" Patrick couldn't imagine not seeing Shannon for months at a time, which would happen if she moved clear across the country.

"He can't leave his mother. She's…sick. Oh, hell, the

woman's a hopeless alcoholic, and she couldn't function without him."

Patrick shoved his hands in his pockets and wished he knew the right thing to say. Probably there wasn't a right thing. "What are you going to do?"

"Think about it. John's coming up for a visit in a few weeks. I guess we'll have to decide then."

"I'd miss you like crazy."

"Hey, I love you," she said.

"Back at you." He'd given her a thumbs-up and sent her on her way.

Before he left, he called the building superintendent at home. "Sorry to bother you, Bert. I'm not sure if you heard, but the aftershock messed up the elevator at city hall."

Bert Wilson sounded gravel-voiced with sleep. "I didn't know about the elevator. I was planning to get in early anyway. I'll do a post-incident property inspection before any of the employees arrive for the day."

"Thanks, Bert. Give me a call if you find anything, will you?"

"You bet."

Patrick would have made do with the leather couch in his outer office for a bed if it weren't for the kids. But there was no way he could let them wake up without him being there when he hadn't been able to tuck them in the night before.

Patrick never pretended to himself or anyone else that he was managing to be both father and mother to his kids, because it wasn't true. He hoped he was doing his best, but with the string of disasters Courage Bay had faced, he'd been home less than he'd liked, even if Janie were still alive. Without her there, he had to rely on his housekeeper and sitters more than he wanted to. He always tried to be home to put Dylan and Fiona to bed, and not to leave for work before they woke. This morning, he was determined to eat breakfast with his children.

As he drove home through the dark, now quiet streets, he was conscious that he'd moved another step away from his wife. For the first time since she'd died, he'd made love to another woman. For all the euphoria that had pumped through his blood when he'd been with Briana, in the back of his mind and heart had been the knowledge that he was breaking another tie to the woman with whom he'd hoped to grow old.

"Oh, Janie," he said into the silence of his car. "I hope I haven't messed things up."

When he'd finally seen Briana in the light after they'd been rescued, he wasn't sure what she was feeling, but it was clear it wasn't all champagne and roses. Of course, she'd looked a little shy when they'd first made eye contact after what they'd shared in the dark elevator, but she'd also looked…troubled.

She'd been as eager as he was in the elevator, though. Briana was the one who'd begged him to fire her temporarily so there'd be no sense of impropriety in what they were doing. Of course, her temporary dismissal was about as legal as a polygamous marriage, but right at that moment, neither of them had worried too much about workplace ethics. She'd wanted him as fiercely as he'd wanted her. What bothered him was afterward. How doggedly she'd insisted on staying on his staff. She was as good as telling him they wouldn't be sleeping together again in the near future.

Patrick was no expert on the subject, but he had a feeling that now that his body had enjoyed sex with a warm and wonderful woman again after three years of celibacy, that same body was going to remind him with annoying frequency that it wanted more—lots and lots more—sex.

If he weren't such a responsible guy, he'd almost have considered quitting his job so he could take his relationship with Briana out into the light. That's how strongly he felt that the two of them could make a future together.

Of course, Briana shouldn't have to quit her job for the sake of their sex life. She'd made it clear that she felt committed to Courage Bay. A sense of duty was rare these days, and that kind of high-minded attitude only made him want her more.

Well, as soon as he got the extra staff and funding that the emergency teams so desperately needed, and as soon as natural disasters started happening somewhere else on the globe for a change, Patrick was going to make sure one of them started looking for a new job.

However, at the moment he couldn't forget about the job he did hold. He drove home by way of the convenience store, his belly knotting when he saw the mess. The roof had caved in, one wall was mostly rubble, and the windows had blown out.

On impulse, he pulled over and stopped the car.

The physical damage didn't worry him so much. Walls and roofs and windows could be replaced. A human life never could.

He recalled the older woman who'd served him and his family. She always had a kind word for the children, and often a couple of lollipops would find their way from the jar she kept behind the till into two eager little fists.

God, the kids could have been there when the shaking began. Anyone's kids could have. The corner store was a popular after-school hangout. If he could be grateful for anything, it would be that there weren't more casualties.

It wasn't much comfort, because even one death was a tragedy, but he'd have been less than human if he didn't say a quick thanks that the children of Courage Bay, including his, were now sleeping peacefully at home.

He drove to his house, then entered as quietly as he could through the door that led from the garage into the laundry room. From there he crept into the kitchen. He headed for Fiona's room first.

His heart squeezed as he gazed down at his little girl. She'd only been two when Janie died, and she didn't remember her mother at all. In sleep she was angelic, her soft brown curls framing her round face, her lips opening and closing slightly as she breathed. She held her favorite stuffed hippo in her arms.

Patrick straightened the covers on her bed, kissed her forehead and went next door to his son's room. Dylan wore baseball pyjamas and had kicked all his covers onto the floor. Patrick picked them up and replaced them, though he knew they'd be back on the floor by morning. He swore his son got more exercise when asleep than he did running around or playing sports.

He tousled the black hair that stuck out in tufts behind Dylan's ears, just as Patrick's had when he was a kid.

Returning to the kitchen, Patrick opened the fridge. Often the housekeeper left him a plate of dinner to microwave if he was late coming home, but since he'd planned to dine with Max Zirinsky, the police chief, there was nothing for him.

Most of the food in the fridge had been bought to appeal to people under the age of ten. Patrick passed on the hot dogs, the gelatin jigglers, the yogurt tubes, the peanut butter and the cheese strings. The mixed tropical fruit juice was no doubt healthy, but right now he didn't want to drink anything quite that color.

Instead, he cracked open a beer, found some crackers and a block of cheddar. He made short work of all three, before taking himself off for the world's quickest shower. In minutes he was falling into bed.

Tomorrow was going to be a hell of a day.

CHAPTER FIVE

PATRICK WALKED into his office next morning at nine, having taken the time to have breakfast with Dylan and Fiona, and to thank Mrs. Simpson for staying the night. She'd had to run home and feed her cat and change clothes before returning for the day.

He knew he could call his parents, or his brother, Sean, or Sean's wife, Linda, to help out when these emergencies arose. They would be there in a flash, if he called. But all of them had their own lives, their own responsibilities. And from the way Dylan and Fiona had climbed all over him and talked his ear off in their excitement to have their father to themselves for a morning, Patrick knew that he was the one his children needed to have around.

Sure, Courage Bay needed him, too, but his kids came first. He pledged right there at the kitchen table over the Cheerios and milk and grapefruit sections that he was going to find more time for Fiona and Dylan.

In his fantasy world, he could work from eight to five and come home to enjoy a civilized family dinner. His job often required him to be out again in the evening for civic meetings, award presentations, any number of social and business functions, but he wanted to be a good father, as well as a good mayor.

In reality, with all the pressures of the past year, it was rare for him to see his kids for more than an hour or two a day, even during the weekends, and that lack of parental involvement was beginning to show in their behavior. The truth was, he could work twenty-four hours a day and still not get everything done either at work or at home.

If only Fiona and Dylan had a mother, he thought, and he had a partner with whom he could share the joys and trials of parenting.

Well, he didn't. If the image of Briana rose to taunt him, he resolutely banished it. He realized now that if she wouldn't leave her position as his admin assistant, there wasn't much of a future for them.

Once Mrs. Simpson returned to the house, he dropped a kiss on Fiona's head. The housekeeper would drop her at her kindergarten class later in the day. He and Dylan got into his car and headed for Dylan's school. Patrick made sure to choose a route that wouldn't take them past the ruined convenience store.

No doubt the collapsed store would be a big topic of discussion at school, but Patrick didn't feel up to explaining to his son that the nice lady who worked at the store had died last night. He didn't trust himself. He was too angry that the emergency response time had been slow. If the paramedics had reached Mrs. Harper sooner, maybe she would have been saved. He didn't want Dylan to pick up on his anger and frustration. Later, when he got home, he'd answer all the questions he knew his kids would pepper him with.

When he arrived at his office, he noted the door was already open and the light on. He wasn't surprised. He'd told Briana to take the morning off, but deep down he'd known she'd ignore the offer. Her work ethic was one of the attributes that made her such a terrific assistant—along with her smarts, her initiative and her ideas.

If it weren't for one big drawback, she'd be perfect for him—the fact he wanted to take their relationship beyond one night in a broken elevator.

Even though he'd known she'd be there, his breath caught in his chest when he entered the open door and saw her at her desk, a phone glued to her ear, and her fingers busily tapping away at a computer keyboard.

Her blond hair was drawn back in an elegant kind of ponytail, and her skin was lightly tanned with a hint of apricot at the cheekbones. She was staring at the screen in front of her, but even from here Patrick could see dark smudges under her eyes. From overwork and lack of sleep, no doubt.

Today she wore a pale green sleeveless cotton blouse that showed off her firm arms. The first button was undone, leaving a respectable vee at the neck, but his gaze traveled down lower, to where her breasts filled out the blouse, breasts he'd kissed so hungrily last night.

His mouth went dry as he stood there, and his mind was filled with remembered sensations. The sound of her helpless panting, the feel of her skin, like warm velvet, the taste of her nipples, hard beneath his tongue.

He'd touched her, inhaled her scent, tasted her—and had no idea what she'd looked like while he did. He was suddenly overcome with a gnawing urge to find out. Were her nipples the color of raspberries? Or apricot, like the blush on her cheeks? Mocha? Caramel? Peaches and cream?

What did the woman he'd so recently made love with look like naked?

He wondered if he'd ever find out.

Perhaps he made a sound, or maybe the intensity of his desire for her caught her attention somehow. Whatever it was, Briana lifted her head and their gazes caught and held. Patrick was tempted to put a hand on the warped oak door frame for support at the impact of her gaze on his nervous system.

The emotions and events of the night before roared back and thickened the atmosphere between them. He felt the sexual tug that had been there from the beginning, only this time it was like a grappling hook.

He knew that for as long as he lived, he'd never forget the expression of conflicted desire in the depths of her luminous eyes, or the struggle he waged with himself not to go over there and haul her into his arms, where she so obviously belonged.

They stayed like that only a few seconds, but it felt like years. Then Briana blinked and said into the phone, "Yes, yes, I'm still here. I'm sorry, what time did you say?"

Her voice was as calmly professional as always, and only the bloom of deeper apricot in her cheeks and her quickened breathing gave away her emotional response to him.

Knowing he'd make a fool of himself—make that a bigger fool of himself—if he stayed there watching her with his tongue hanging out, he walked by her desk with his best imitation of a casual wave and entered his own office.

Already a stack of pink message slips awaited him. Four of the five city councilors had called. Cecil Thomson was the only one who hadn't bothered.

Patrick's mother, Mary O'Shea, had called. Damn. He'd meant to phone her this morning to let her know he and the kids were fine. She'd be checking in with all her family this morning if he knew his mom, reassuring herself that all her brood were safe. No doubt she'd heard about him being stuck in the elevator, and since the radio and television news had both reported on the damage in town, she'd have seen the collapsed convenience store and worried about its proximity to his home.

He picked up the phone to call her, only to be interrupted. Briana buzzed him on the intercom to let him know that the building superintendent was here to see him.

"Bert," he said, rising and extending his hand. "How's it going?"

"Not too bad. I've done the postincident property inspection and we're in pretty good shape." Bert glanced down at his printed checklist. "The vibrating caused a short in the elevator, that's why it stuck. The fire crew didn't do much damage when they got you out, but the elevator company's coming to fix the door-closure arms and reset the circuitry. They should be through by noon."

Patrick nodded. "That's good then. No other damage?"

"No," Bert said. "City hall's solidly built, no question. But we should consider seismic upgrades to the suspended ceiling and light fixtures on all floors. If we do it floor by floor, we can minimize the disruption."

"That's a good idea, Bert. Put together a report and include a budget. Let's see what we can do. I have to be honest, though. We've got more urgent expense items for Courage Bay's already overstretched budget. We're probably looking at next year."

Bert didn't seem surprised. "I'll put together the report anyway."

Once he left, Briana brought in more message slips. Reporters from the *Sentinel* and the local TV and radio stations had called. They'd want to know about his stint in the trapped elevator, no doubt, and also, he suspected, how the municipal government was planning to support Courage Bay. He blew out a breath, dragged off his suit jacket, loosened the tie he'd put on not an hour ago, and picked up the phone. Before he had a chance to do more than hit the first number, his intercom buzzed. "Yeah."

"It's Dan Egan on the phone," she said. "He wants to see you today."

Who didn't? He respected and liked the fire chief, but right now he didn't have time for a diatribe. "Look, Briana, I know he's shorthanded and I'm about to start calling an emergency council meeting. I'll let him know the minute—"

"I don't think he's calling about funding," she said, her voice sounding concerned even over the intercom. "He says it's important, and he must know you of all people are aware of his staffing shortages."

If there were two people in the world who wouldn't waste his time, they were Briana and Dan Egan. If both of them thought he needed this meeting, he'd be there. "Okay. Set it up."

He flicked through the messages once more. He'd pass the media ones on to Archie Weld and let him deal with them for now.

Then he called his mom to let her know he was fine. He was secretly relieved to hear his dad's recorded voice telling him to leave a message, which he did, knowing it was a lot quicker than talking to his mother in person.

While he checked his e-mail and made the few calls he needed to return, anger drummed dully behind his eyeballs. Courage Bay's emergency services needed a funding boost and he needed council's approval to give it to them.

Wondering how soon he could set up an emergency council meeting, he picked up his schedule, which sat in its usual place on the edge of his desk. Briana, as he'd known she would, had already rearranged things to give him some time in the office this morning.

His first function was a ribbon-cutting at a seniors' residence that had been badly damaged during a recent fire.

For a second he contemplated canceling, then paused, as he imagined Briana must have done, and considered the importance of his presence. Patrick wasn't any Roosevelt or Churchill; he was the mayor of a city of eighty-five thousand. However, he was still a politician and a community leader. He'd always admired men who set an example of integrity and cheer when times were tough.

And times in Courage Bay were tough indeed.

This seniors' residence was symbolic of the city. It had been hurt, but like the people who lived here, it had come through the bad times. And Patrick needed to be there to help celebrate that fact. Besides, he'd given his word to the organizers that he'd attend, and he didn't like going back on his word.

Other than that, Briana had managed to clear his calendar. She'd penciled in a couple of suggestions, though. A rescheduled meeting with Max being one of them.

He nodded, even though there was no one in the room to see. One of the many things he liked about Briana was her initiative. She'd become more than an assistant to him in the past couple of months. She was more like a partner, and it bothered him that he was getting credit for a lot of her work.

Even if he didn't have his own reasons for doing so, he'd be trying to help her move up to a position where she could shine and have a chance to use her talents to their fullest.

"Patrick?"

He glanced up sharply and there she was in the doorway. Her tone was almost hesitant as she stood there, and once more that arc of heat stretched between them when their gazes locked.

"Briana..." His own voice came out husky.

"I...um..." She made a motion to push her hair back behind her ear, obviously forgetting that her hair was tied back. He liked her uncertainty; it made him hope she'd been as deeply affected by last night as he had. She dropped her hand when she realized her hair was already neatly tied behind her head and said, "I scheduled a meeting with Dan Egan for ten-thirty this morning."

He nodded and watched her walk forward and take his schedule, then write in the meeting and the location. Dan's office. Good. It would give him a chance to check on Shannon, see how she was doing after last night's fatal blaze.

Briana passed him his copy of his schedule, and he thought the computer printout trembled slightly in her hands. As he took it from her, he caught a faint whiff of lavender.

"About your ribbon-cutting at noon," she began.

"You were absolutely right to leave it scheduled. I'm damn sick and tired of putting off celebration in this town. Besides, I said I'd go and I stick to my word."

She blinked at him and he grinned. "Sorry, I probably sound like my dad, but he always taught us never to lie, and never to go back on our word. I try to follow those rules."

There was a crease between her brows as though she didn't believe him. Or maybe she was worrying about him making both the meeting and the ribbon-cutting when things were so crazy.

"I believe in telling the truth, too," she said softly. "But sometimes people can make mistakes. I think if a person does that, they should speak up and rectify the situation, don't you?" Her eyes burned with a significance he couldn't interpret.

He nodded, wondering what she was getting at.

"If a person's hurt another person, they should admit that, even if it's difficult at the time," she elaborated.

She wasn't speaking rhetorically here. He felt quite sure she was sending him a message.

Suddenly he felt as though the building might be experiencing another aftershock. The world didn't seem stable beneath his feet.

"Did I hurt you?" he asked urgently. He'd been so eager last night, so lost in lust and, frankly, so out of practice that maybe he'd done something to hurt her. If so, he'd never forgive himself.

Her cheeks flamed. "No. Of course you didn't hurt me."

"Then what are you talking about?"

"Nothing. Forget I spoke. I was speaking in general terms." She pulled away from the desk and would have moved on to the next item of business, of which he knew there was plenty, but he stopped her.

"Briana, we can't pretend nothing happened last night. I think we should talk about it."

Amusement flickered across her face and caused her eyes to twinkle. "*We should talk about it* is supposed to be the woman's line."

"Well, based on the way you've reverted to all business, I'm guessing I'd wait a long time for you to open the subject."

She huffed out a breath and he saw for a moment the vulnerability and sadness behind the external efficiency.

"I don't think this is the appropriate time or place for such a discussion." He opened his mouth to argue, but she went on. "What happened was—"

"Incredible."

Warmth lit her eyes as she gazed at him briefly, before returning her attention to the printed schedule in her hand. "Yes. It was. But it was also—"

"Inappropriate. I know that, Briana. But the thing is, it happened, and all the pretending in the world won't make it *un*-happen."

"No."

"I want to see you again," he said urgently.

She looked at him as though that was bad news for some reason. "You do."

"Damn right I do. Maybe nights like that happen all the time for you, but they don't for me." He might be out of practice sexually, but he knew damn well that it wasn't just the sex but the intimacy, the…something special between them that had made it such a stand-out experience. He doubted very much that she'd ever had a night like that any more than he had.

"No—"

"I didn't think so. The thing is—"

His phone began to shrill. Even as he told her to leave it, she was leaning over him to pick up the receiver. "Mayor's office."

He watched, frustrated, as she said, "Right. Yes. Of course. I'll tell him."

But her next words pushed all thoughts of his personal life out of his head. Briana looked sad and troubled. "Patty Reese, the woman from the basement suite fire, died in hospital this morning."

"Shit."

"Yes."

For now, Patrick realized, he and Briana were going to have to put their personal lives aside and concentrate on running this town.

Briana left and he spent the next hour returning calls, making a statement for the paper, and going over his notes for the ribbon-cutting ceremony. But he was thinking of his sister Shannon's exhausted expression the night before. Of the valiant and ultimately futile effort to save Patty Reese.

CHAPTER SIX

WHILE PATRICK was busy in his office, Briana received a call from her uncle Cecil.

"I heard about what happened last night," he said as soon as he'd identified himself.

Her heart sank. Somehow, she'd hoped no one would find out about her forced confinement with her boss. If Uncle Cecil knew, he was no doubt wondering if she'd made good use of her time and obtained evidence to incriminate her boss.

Well, she wasn't going to tell anyone what had happened last night. She'd been crazy to tape their lovemaking, crazier still to think she could make love with a man and then betray him.

"Look, Uncle—"

"Your aunt and I have been worried sick. Are you all right? I phoned your home first. I can't believe you're at work. You should go to the hospital and get checked out. I'll come and get you."

She smiled into the phone. He wasn't even thinking about her mission. He was worried about her. It was nice to be fussed over, even if it was unnecessary. "I'm fine, really. I should have phoned you this morning to let you know I was all right. I'm sorry. I didn't realize you'd worry."

"Of course we worry about you, honey. You're the closest to a daughter we've got."

"I know. Thanks. But I wasn't hurt at all in the elevator." Well, not physically anyway. She suspected her heart might be in danger, though.

"Why don't you come for dinner tonight. Irene will look after you. You can stay over in the guest room if you like."

So far, she'd been careful not to be seen too much in her aunt and uncle's company, since no one was to know about their relationship. They must really be worried about her. She was touched by their love. "I'd love to come for dinner. I'll stay at my own place, though."

"Whatever you say. But at least go to your doctor and make sure everything's fine." He blew out a breath. "When I think of what could have happened if that cable had snapped...."

"It didn't, though. I'm fine. How about you? Were you both all right?"

"Oh, yes. We were watching TV and everything shook for a few seconds. That was it."

"I'm glad to hear it. Well, thanks for calling. I'm sorry you and Aunt Irene were worried. See you tonight."

She sat for a couple of minutes simply staring at her computer screen but not seeing it.

The tape was like an unexploded land mine sitting there in her purse. She'd been crazy to record what had happened last night. Not only crazy, but devious. She'd destroy the tape today and try to talk to her uncle at dinner about the possibility that Patrick wasn't the one who'd set him up.

In two months, she hadn't seen him act with anything but integrity. Even last night, it had been Patrick who'd tried to call a halt to their lovemaking. She'd been the aggressor in the end. That tape was history.

She listened carefully for a minute. She could hear Patrick on the phone and knew she had time to take out the tape and destroy it.

Grabbing her bag, she dug into it. Where was the damn tape recorder?

Looking inside the bag didn't help. Had the recorder somehow become wedged at the bottom? A flutter of panic started in her chest. She dumped her bag upside down on her desktop and shook it. A small avalanche of keys, wallet, cell phone, half a roll of mints, lip gloss and makeup bag tumbled out, along with the small silk bag that had come in so handy last night, a quarter and two pennies.

Frantic, she scrambled through the stuff. The tape recorder had to be here. She hadn't touched it since last night.

Biting her lip, she decided it must have fallen out in her car or at home.

Her intercom buzzed. "Briana? Can you come in here for a moment?"

"Sure." She shoved everything back into her bag and tucked it out of sight, then took her notebook and entered the adjoining office. Patrick was behind the desk, working up some notes in his angular handwriting.

"Can you organize an emergency council meeting for tonight?"

"Tonight?" she asked. After stonewalling Patrick's efforts to increase the emergency team's budget, council might be more receptive after this latest disaster. But calling a meeting the day after was almost unheard of.

"It's important."

"Yes. Of course," she said. "Seven o'clock?"

He rubbed his jaw. "Make it eight. I've barely seen my kids in the last week."

She nodded, hearing the bleakness in his voice and doing her best to offer comfort. "At least you let them call you at work when they need you. A lot of fathers wouldn't do that."

He made a sound of irritation in his throat. "A lot of fathers would see their kids more than an hour a day, too. If it weren't for our housekeeper, I don't know what I'd do."

"Isn't there anyone else who could help out? Family?"

"My family do their best, but they're all busy, too. My wife's parents retired to Florida. We see them a couple of times a year, but they're not close enough to be much help." He forced a smile. "We do okay. Once things settle down around Courage Bay, my job will be a lot easier."

With a soundless sigh, she went back to her own desk, picked up her phone and started calling the councilors. Because he was on her mind, she called her uncle, Cecil Thomson, first.

When his secretary at the bank answered, she was put right through. "Yes, Briana," her uncle replied. "What can I do for you?"

"The mayor has called an emergency council meeting tonight at 8:00 p.m."

"I see. What's this all about?"

Briana knew her uncle's secretary must be in the room, or he would have grilled her further. "I'll be faxing out an agenda later this afternoon."

"Well…" She knew her uncle wanted to refuse, not only because he hated the mayor but because he'd have phoned Aunt Irene immediately to let her know Briana was coming for dinner.

"I'm sorry to hear that. I had dinner plans, but I guess I'll have to cancel them…?"

"I think that would be best," she agreed, knowing she'd be busy putting together info packets and preparing for the council meeting. She'd be lucky to get dinner at all.

Briana was on the phone with Councilor Gwendolyn Clark a short time later, when Patrick strode out of the office, pulling on his jacket as he went. He waved goodbye, and she raised her hand back at him, then watched hungrily as he left, trying not to remember what that tall, athletic body had felt like last night.

Please, let him be innocent so I can love him. The direction of her thoughts almost caused her to fall out of her office chair. *Love?* What was wrong with her? Patrick was a nice man and a wonderful lover. But who said anything about love?

PATRICK WALKED down the main stairs at city hall deep in thought. He'd gone over the city budget again this morning. He bet he knew that complex document as well as the city treasurer did. There was money available. Courage Bay wasn't bankrupt. They had a couple of million in secured savings. There was no specific purpose for the money; it existed so that Courage Bay would never go bankrupt, and to cover any extraordinary expenses.

Well, if bumping up the emergency forces after the year

they'd had wasn't an extraordinary need, Patrick didn't know what was. The money was set up as a trust, designed to be pilfer-proof and wisely spent. A one hundred percent yes vote by council was required before any expenditure could be approved. In order to draw more than half a million dollars from the fund in any one year, a city plebiscite was required, a referendum whereby the citizens of Courage Bay could decide how they wanted their money spent.

He intended to try one more time at tonight's meeting to get the full vote of council to free up some of those funds for the emergency teams.

The noise of a power drill reminded him that the elevator repairs were under way. He headed over for a second to see how they were going. Bert was there and obviously knew one of the two men at work. "Here's the man who spent several hours in your fine elevator last night," Bert joked as Patrick came closer.

He nodded to both men. The one who'd been chatting with Bert said, "Well, you were never in any danger. We've checked the elevator out thoroughly. Should have it back in operation within the hour."

Bert crossed the foyer to speak to a passing file clerk and Patrick thanked the two men for their quick response time. "No problem," said Bert's acquaintance, turning back to his drill.

The second man emerged from inside the elevator and said, "Did Bert say you were the guy stuck in here last night?"

"That's right," Patrick confirmed.

"This must be yours, then," the worker said, holding out a small silver tape recorder.

"Yes it is." Patrick recognized the small recorder. "It must have fallen out of my briefcase."

The elevator repairman handed the tape recorder over and Patrick dropped it into his case. With a final thanks to the two men and a wave to Bert, he headed out for his meeting with Dan Egan.

Since he fully believed that part of his job was to be a leader in times of crisis, Patrick stowed his grim mood as he pulled up in front of the Jefferson Avenue firehouse and got out of his car.

"Hey, Patrick!" he was hailed by Louis Alvarez, an engineer with squad two.

After joking for a few minutes with Louis and his squad members, Patrick said, "Came to see the chief."

"He's in his office."

That was unusual. Dan Egan was more of a man's man than a paper-pusher, and whenever possible, he preferred to be out with his men and away from his desk. As Patrick looked around at the faces of the firefighters, he saw how fatigued they all appeared and was determined to get the funding that would lighten their load.

"Where's my kid sister?" he said, already having noted that Shannon wasn't out front.

"I saw her with Bud Patchett a couple minutes ago."

He nodded. If she'd been trapped by the garrulous firehouse mechanic, it could be days before anyone saw her. For a second Patrick missed the camaraderie and hard physical work of the firehouse. The blazes these guys fought were real smoke-and-flame jobs, not the insidious political fires that wasted so much of Patrick's time and energy.

Shaking off the momentary nostalgia, he made his way

back to his former office, which looked almost exactly as it had in his day, except the pictures of Janie and the kids were gone, and it was a different guy behind the desk.

At the moment, though, Dan Egan wasn't behind his desk. He was standing with Sam Prophet and both men looked grim.

"What's up?" Patrick asked as he entered the room.

Chief Egan, a Texan with a big smile and a hearty laugh, didn't offer a hand to shake or an easy word, merely an unsmiling nod.

Sam Prophet, the arson investigator, didn't look any happier.

Patrick got a bad feeling in his gut. Taking his cue from the heavy atmosphere in the room, he closed the office door behind him.

"You said you had something important to discuss?" Patrick asked.

"That's right," Chief Egan said. "Show him, Sam."

Prophet reached onto the desk for a plastic evidence box and handed it to Patrick.

He looked inside, careful not even to breathe on the twisted and charred scraps of plastic inside. A bit of charred wire also sat in the box.

"The remains of a cell phone," Prophet said in a clipped tone. "I found it this morning when I went through the basement suite that burned down last night. This is what caused the fire that killed Patty Reese. Someone packed the phone with explosives, and then dialed the number, setting off the device."

"Have you confirmed traces of explosives?" Patrick asked.

"I haven't sent this into the lab yet, but I'd bet my pension on it. We've seen this M.O. before. Dan and I have named the bastard The Trigger."

"We're going to get that bastard. I swear to you, Patrick, that we are going to get him." Dan's slow Texas drawl was filled with disgust.

"But not without more resources." Patrick heard the edge of fury in his own voice.

"Hey, we know you're doing everything you can," Dan said. "I've sat in those damn council meetings. Nobody's blaming you."

But Patrick was. It was still his responsibility as mayor of this town to see that the city ran smoothly. What a laugh. When he thought back to his early days of campaigning, he'd imagined there'd be nothing more required of him than that he perform his job with integrity and fiscal responsibility.

Who could have foreseen that within months of him taking office, his town would face a host of natural and human foes. Would he go back and change his place in all of this if he could?

No, by God, he wouldn't. He'd been voted in by the people of this town, not the council, and if the council wouldn't see reason, maybe he was going to have to go straight to the citizens of Courage Bay.

An idea was beginning to form.

"Sam," he said, "how long until the media gets hold of this?"

"You mean that the fire last night was arson?"

"Yeah."

Sam gave a tight smile. "Well, I'm not going to tell them—at least not until the tests are completed. Right now, we haven't got so much as a lead on the guy. All you have is my hunch."

It was more than a hunch and they all knew it. But Sam was also right that they couldn't go public until the test results were in.

"I've called an emergency council meeting planned for tonight to try and get five heads out of five asses," Patrick said. "If I don't succeed, I'm upping the pressure on council. You guys need the resources to get to the bottom of this."

Sam took the evidence box and carefully replaced it in his leather case. "I'll get right on it." He glanced at Patrick. "Anything you can do to help us catch this guy means..." He cracked a grin. "You get my vote for mayor next time around."

Happy to help lighten the grim mood, Patrick said, "I thought I got your vote last time."

"You did," Sam conceded. "Okay, you help us get the resources to catch The Trigger and you'll get both my vote in the next election and a beer."

Patrick chuckled. "Don't you know better than to attempt to bribe a city official? I'll buy my own beer. But thanks."

The two men shook hands and Sam left the office.

"Leave the door open," Dan said. Turning to Patrick, he explained, "I like to be available for any of the guys."

"Speaking of which, here's one of the 'guys' now," Patrick said, raising an eyebrow at his chauvinist friend. Shannon was on her way to the office with the fire mechanic, Bud Patchett, in tow.

"No, really, Shannon. No need to bother the chief. I was just letting off some steam," they heard Patchett say as Shannon pretty much manhandled him into the chief's office.

If Shannon wasn't with the mechanic, Patrick might plead an urgent appointment and hustle out of there. Bud Patchett could talk.

"Hey, bro," she said, seeing Patrick. "You okay after last night?"

Whether she was referring to the elevator ordeal or to his intimacy with Briana, which Shannon had obviously guessed at, he didn't know. But he decided to assume she meant the elevator. "I'm fine. You guys did a great job, thanks."

"That's what we're here for," she said. She smiled at him, but there were lines of fatigue around her eyes, and knowing Shannon, she'd have taken the death of Patty Reese hard.

He might be the mayor and she might be a firefighter, but he was still her big brother. "I'm sorry Ms. Reese didn't make it, kid."

Shannon nodded. "Yeah. Me, too."

For a moment no one spoke, then she seemed to pull herself together. "Bud here has something to say to you, Dan, and maybe since you're here, you ought to hear it too, Patrick."

"I didn't know the mayor was here. Hello, Patrick."

"Hi, Bud. Don't mind me. If you've got something to say, go ahead and say it."

The mechanic glanced back and forth between the fire chief and the mayor, finally addressing his remarks to the chief. "Dan, I'm sorry to add to your troubles today, but I've got to get some more maintenance help. Our trucks have been used to full capacity in the past weeks. They need more frequent maintenance, and one of the guys said there was a small leak in the spare fire hose. I need another part-timer at least."

Dan nodded, his gaze fixed on the mechanic. One of the reasons Patrick respected his replacement as fire chief was the way Egan listened to his people. Bud knew his way around a fire engine better than anyone, and if he said he needed more help, then he did.

The familiar burn of anger intensified in Patrick's belly. Damn it, it was his job to make sure the fire crews had the resources they needed, right down to enough guys to check the brakes regularly.

"Let me see what I can do, Bud," Dan said. "In the meantime, I appreciate knowing you're doing your best."

"Yes, sir. I do my very best. I love those engines. And I like to see them running smooth and polished to a shine."

Patrick knew they had more to worry about than shiny fire trucks. They had a murderous arsonist to catch, and it was his job as mayor to find the funding to ensure they stopped the killer.

CHAPTER SEVEN

PATRICK ARRIVED at the ribbon-cutting ceremony with a few minutes to spare. He pulled out his cell phone and returned one of the messages he hadn't had time for this morning.

"Archie Weld," the deep voice answered. Archie had spent twenty years in radio before taking the job as media liaison for city hall.

"Archie, Patrick O'Shea."

"Patrick, as I'm sure you know, everybody wants a statement, they want an interview, they want pictures, footage, a reenactment of the mayor's incarceration in his own elevator."

Patrick chuckled. "I hear you. Look, Archie, can you tell them all I'll cooperate fully, but not today. I'm sure even our media friends can appreciate I've got a lot to do today. If you want to put together some kind of release giving the details of what happened and that no one in city hall was hurt, go ahead and put some quotes in from me. If you e-mail it to Briana, she'll make sure I read it and get it back to you this afternoon."

"I think the TV and papers want—"

"Pictures. They'll get them, but not until tomorrow. Look, I've got something going on and I want to do a live appearance on the six o'clock news tomorrow night. Can you set it up?"

"Sure."

"I appreciate it."

"Uh, Patrick, it's going to be easier to get the station to agree with this if they know what it's about."

"I've got an important message for the people of this city, but I don't want to say more until tomorrow. I'll fill you in later, but sell the TV guys on the concept, will you? You'll think of something."

"I'll do my best."

"Once I finish the on-air broadcast, I'll take a full media conference. Everyone can have pictures, sound bites, full interviews, whatever they need. I think I can promise the show will be…interesting. Probably dramatic."

"I hope you know what you're doing."

"Thanks. So do I."

"If you want me to prepare you some speaking notes—"

"Nope. I'm going to wing it."

"Okay, it's your funeral."

Actually, he was hoping to prevent a few funerals. There had been too many in Courage Bay.

BRIANA WAS THE FIRST to arrive at the council chambers located on the main floor of city hall. Since this was an in-camera meeting, there were no spectators in the visitors' seating area.

It was quiet yet, the only sound a soft plunk as Briana dropped an agenda package in front of each person's place. The package included the agenda, which was pretty short, since Patrick only had one order of business, and the attached budgets and expense records of the city's emergency crews. She'd been shocked at how much money had been spent on extra staffing to cover injured emergency personnel, on maintenance and upkeep for all the equipment, and on overtime.

It was clear even to a noneconomist like herself that the city's budget was stretched to the max and soon they'd have overspent for the year, yet still the emergency services needed more money, and urgently.

The final item was a printout of the rules regarding the city's financial safety net. A sizeable bond to be accessed only in times of emergency.

Even though she knew that her uncle had been instrumental in turning down the mayor's repeated requests for more funding, Briana was certain that after he'd read the latest update, Cecil would be one of the first to vote for additional funding.

Their city needed it desperately.

A few minutes before the meeting was to start, everyone was there but Uncle Cecil. He never missed a council meeting. Surely he'd be here?

Patrick took his place at the head of the horseshoe-shaped table promptly at 8:00 p.m. Her uncle's place was still empty.

Patrick glanced pointedly at the empty seat and then at his watch. "We'll give Councilman Thomson five minutes, and then we'll begin without him," Patrick said, though of course she knew it would be all but pointless, since he needed a unanimous yes vote by council in order to access the funds.

She heard footsteps echoing on the marble floor, heading for the door that led to the council chambers. Briana let out the breath she'd been holding.

Her uncle entered and walked to his place at the table and sat down. He made eye contact with no one, simply picked up the package in front of him and glanced through it, even though Briana had personally sent copies of all the documents out to all the council members earlier in the day.

She sat at the table reserved for staff along with council assistant Lorna Sinke and Archie Weld. She'd suggested Fire Chief Dan Egan and Police Chief Max Zirinsky be asked to attend, but Patrick had vetoed the idea. "They're too busy to get tangled up in bureaucracy," he'd said. "The numbers are in the budgets and speak for themselves."

But now that she saw the expressions ranging from boredom to hostility on the faces of the councilmen and councilwoman, she wasn't so sure he was right. Max and Dan could both give powerful, passionate presentations on behalf of their departments. Although, since they were both strongly opinionated, never backed down from a fight and loathed red tape, Briana could also appreciate Patrick's strategy in having them absent.

"Thank you all for coming," Patrick began. "I'm sorry to pull you away from other plans, but I think you'll agree that matters have gone from serious to critical. As you'll see from the enclosed budgets, both projected and actual, the fire department is twenty-eight percent overbudget for the year, police seventeen percent and existing services are stretched to the limit."

The sounds of papers shuffling could be heard as the councilors flipped through to the budget pages in their handouts. A frown creased Councilman Ed Prescott's brow and he glanced at Cecil Thomson. Ed Prescott was one of Uncle Cecil's supporters on council. The owner of a local pharmacy, he was always concerned about costs.

Uncle Cecil had been on council the longest. Both Ed Prescott and Councilman Gerald Anderson had supported his unsuccessful bid for mayor and it was clear that he still had their support. They usually deferred to Cecil's opinion, and that gave the three of them a majority vote on a council of five. Cecil might not be the mayor, but he wielded a lot of power behind the scenes.

"Mr. Mayor," said Councilman Prescott, "we've had this discussion before. At the time, we voted not to increase the city budgets. I'm not sure why we're having this meeting at all."

Briana glanced at Patrick and saw his jaw tense. He let a moment pass before answering, and she could only imagine the retorts he had to swallow before he came out with a respectable response. "Since our last meeting, Councilman Prescott, we've had a further emergency situation in which two more of our citizens died.

"I had discussions today with both Fire Chief Dan Egan and Police Chief Max Zirinsky, and while they are not saying both fatalities could have been avoided with larger budgets, there is no question that their resources are stretched beyond what is reasonable. We need to give them the money to do their jobs."

A hand went up. It was Uncle Cecil's other longtime supporter, Councilman Gerald Anderson, an attorney in his late sixties known for his conservative views.

"While your concern is certainly laudable," the councilman said, "and I know we all admire the fine job our men and women in the EMS have been doing, I'm wondering, where are you proposing we get the money?"

Patrick looked up directly at Briana. She knew what he was thinking as clearly as though she could read his mind. If ever a man was about to blow, Patrick was that man. He let his gaze rest on her for a moment and she smiled slightly, letting him know silently that she was with him in this fight.

He gave an imperceptible nod and turned to answer the councilman. "There is only one place we can get the money, Councilman Anderson. We would have to take it from the city bond, which, I might remind you, was set up to support the people of this city in times of need. I can think of few times when the city has been in greater need."

There was a pause.

Uncle Cecil raised his hand and Patrick acknowledged him.

"Mayor O'Shea…" Her uncle paused to give the mayor and the rest of council a broad smile. Briana eased back in her chair and relaxed. It was going to be okay. Uncle Cecil was going to side with Patrick, and she knew he had enough clout on council that his vote would sway the others.

Uncle Cecil was a big man. He'd played football in college and still kept himself in good shape. He was handsome, with silver hair and warm blue eyes. But it was his charm that was his greatest asset, she thought. Charm and an air of command.

"We certainly appreciate what you are trying to do here, Mayor. We understand you've been a fireman yourself and know how hard our men and women are working to keep this city safe."

There was general nodding, and Briana found herself nodding along with everyone else. Except Patrick, who was looking at Uncle Cecil with an impassive expression on his face.

"And our police and SWAT team, the ambulance services and the paramedics have done as fine a job as any group of men and women ever did," Cecil continued. "However, some of us have been on this council a lot of years." He glanced modestly around the room, but everyone knew he'd been there longest of them all, and had Patrick not won a surprise election, Cecil Thomson would be leading them today. "We've seen trouble come and go, young man."

She glanced at Patrick to see how he was taking the "young man" comment, but while his gaze had hardened, and his lips were set tight together, he still showed an implacable countenance.

"It's easy to panic in times of crisis, and no one thinks any the less of you for believing more money is going to solve our problems. But, son, money can't stop earthquakes, or fires, or floods or any other natural disasters. When they happen, the emergency teams are going to be stretched, naturally. But then we'll experience our usual periods of calm. During those times, we'll recoup those losses you're so concerned about."

Cecil spread his hands and glanced around the room. "If we spend the money every time we have a few unfortunate tragedies, well, we'll soon find ourselves broke."

"That money was set aside for disaster relief," Patrick said in a hard tone.

"Exactly. And if a true disaster strikes and the money's

spent, it will be too late. We've had some tough times in the last few months, I'm not denying it, son...." Briana gritted her teeth on Patrick's behalf. She knew Uncle Cecil was calling him "son" deliberately and it wasn't fair. "But we've got to hang on to our rainy day fund, not squander it on a drizzle."

Patrick did his best. He argued passionately for council to release the money. She saw Fred Glazeman, one of the kindest men she knew, nodding a few times as Patrick spoke. However, Briana sensed that Councilwoman Gwendolyn Clark, the niece of one of Courage Bay's most respected judges, was swayed by Uncle Cecil's arguments.

"I understand you're upset, Mayor O'Shea," her uncle resumed. "We're all upset that more lives were lost in our city, but let's not be too quick to run out and spend money that we can't replace once it's gone. Let's let things set for a month. If, as I fully expect, the city returns to its normal peaceful state, then we won't have spent emergency money needlessly." He paused and looked slowly around the room at each of the councilmen in turn. "However, if at that time, we feel we need to broach that bond, we can vote on it then."

Patrick spoke again and his voice was less calm this time. "I urge you all to ask yourselves how you would feel if it were your sister or mother or wife who'd perished yesterday because the fire crews were so stretched they couldn't reach both women in time to save them."

"Son, even the one they did save died," Uncle Cecil reminded him. "It's a tragedy, but not every tragedy can be averted with money."

"It's worth our while to try and prevent every tragedy,"

Patrick countered. He looked round the table, making eye contact with each councilman or woman in turn, then said, "Do you want more deaths on your conscience?"

The vote was called, and as Briana had feared, it wasn't unanimous.

"Motion not carried," said Patrick in a clipped tone. There was little more to say, and in minutes the meeting was adjourned.

Briana felt as if somebody had kicked her in the stomach. She'd worked all day preparing the irrefutable evidence that there was an acute funding shortage in the city, and Patrick had argued passionately and eloquently on behalf of the very people who risked their lives day after day to keep Courage Bay safe.

How could they have failed?

Maybe Uncle Cecil would have voted against the proposal no matter who was mayor, but she couldn't get out of her mind the possibility that her uncle had let personal feelings interfere with his better judgment.

She left as soon as she could. As she glanced back, she saw that Patrick was talking with the two councilors who'd supported him. Her uncle and his two supporters left chambers together. Her uncle glanced her way and, when no one was looking, winked at her. She smiled slightly, but couldn't rid herself of the weight of disappointment that pressed on her chest.

She knew Uncle Cecil was a fiscal conservative, and she respected his views. She only wished he could be a little more open to the fact that this current funding crisis wasn't a little blip. Courage Bay was practically fighting for its life. In the past months the city had faced drought, severe storms, forest fires, earthquakes, mud slides and a rare viral outbreak. Now it seemed their latest crisis would be a monetary one.

She would have liked to exchange a word with Patrick, just to let him know how sorry she was his motion hadn't passed, but he was busy chatting with Fred Glazeman when she left.

In no mood to go straight home, in spite of a sleepless night followed by a marathon day at work, she headed for Uncle Cecil and Aunt Irene's place. Maybe she could do more good for this city if she could reconcile her uncle to Patrick's proposal. If she could get Cecil Thomson onside, she knew he'd sway those who'd voted with him. She smiled wryly. She'd gone from undercover spy to lobbyist in one day.

Not that she was much of a spy. Her only piece of evidence was missing. At lunchtime she'd checked her car thoroughly, and even casually asked Bert if he'd found anything in the elevator. He'd handed her a paper clip and made some joke about recycling office supplies. Hah, hah.

She'd even phoned Shannon O'Shea to see if the firefighters had picked up anything, though common sense told her they'd have handed the tape recorder over right away if they had found it.

"What have you lost?" Shannon asked.

"Just an earring. It wasn't valuable, but it has sentimental value."

"Did you ask Patrick?" Shannon queried, an edge to her voice, and Briana wished she hadn't bothered phoning. The tape and recorder must be at home somewhere.

Her aunt was delighted to see her. Irene Thomson was

a very attractive woman who always looked elegant. Even her white slacks and sky-blue blouse were dressed up with an expensive leather belt and loafers. She'd let her hair go gray and it was a gorgeous pewter color, stunning against her porcelain complexion and deep blue eyes.

After wrapping her niece in a scented embrace, she insisted on warming up some leftover dinner. "If I know you, you've been too busy to eat properly. I know Cecil will be hungry when he gets home."

So Briana found herself sipping sparkling water and putting a bowl of salad on the already set table when her uncle walked in. He broke into a big smile when he saw her and, after he'd kissed his wife hello, wrapped his niece in a bear hug. "So, you came for dinner after all," he said lightly.

"I didn't plan to eat, but Aunt Irene loves to feed me."

He chuckled. "That she does."

Over dinner they chatted about the family and reminisced about a holiday the three of them had taken in France and Italy as a present to Briana when she'd graduated from college. By the time they'd finished dinner, they were laughing heartily.

"It was all right for you two, but I had an awful time fighting off the men who went wild over Briana," her uncle complained.

"I think it was my blond hair," Briana said, wrinkling her nose.

"Nonsense. You're too beautiful for your own good. You take after your mother that way."

"Oh, that was such a good trip. Why don't I get out the photo albums?" Aunt Irene suggested.

"I was really hoping to talk to Uncle Cecil for a few minutes about a work thing," Briana said.

"Oh, of course, dear. I'm sure you've got lots to discuss." Her aunt didn't take an active role in Briana's deception, but Briana knew Irene felt no compunction about hurting the man who'd hurt her husband. Briana understood that kind of loyalty. She had it herself. The trouble was, as loyal as she was to her uncle, she was fast developing an equally strong loyalty to her boss.

Uncle Cecil took her into his study. The room's decor was inspired by a traditional men's club. Burgundy walls, a British India rug, an oversize mahogany desk, leather chairs and even hunting prints on the walls.

She almost expected to be offered a cigar and brandy when she sat down.

"Uncle Cecil," she said, "I've been working for Patrick O'Shea for two months now and he's never done anything remotely illegal or unethical."

Her uncle's eyes hardened and his mouth firmed. "What about inappropriate overtures to his assistant?"

Forcing herself not to blush, she shook her head. It was the truth, after all. She was the one who'd made the overtures in the elevator.

"I see. Well, he's been busy." Cecil blew out a breath. "We've all been busy with this wretched trouble."

"I know. I'm just wondering. Uncle Cecil, could it have been someone else who sent that false evidence to the *Sentinel*?"

"Of course not. Who else would bother?"

"I know it sounds strange, but maybe someone who supported his campaign?"

Uncle Cecil leaned back in his chair and regarded the ceiling, his habit when he was thinking deeply. "You're suggesting Zirinsky could have acted on his own?"

Max Zirinsky was a good man. It was difficult to imagine him doing something so underhanded. "I'm only saying that it might not have been Patrick O'Shea. And if it wasn't him," she hurried on, "then maybe you two could bury the hatchet and try working together for the good of Courage Bay."

Her uncle turned to look at her, and she saw the hurt in his eyes. "Do you think I don't care about this city? I've lived here most of my life. I know these people. I've served them both as a banker and as a councilor. It's my duty to stop some young hothead with dubious ethics and his own agenda from spending us into bankruptcy. I won't let him destroy this city, Briana. I won't."

"Are you sure this isn't personal?" she asked softly.

"Of course, it's personal. He ruined my chances of ever being mayor, he ruined my loving wife's peace of mind for weeks. Now it looks like your precious mayor is trying to ruin my relationship with my niece!"

"I just want to do the right thing," she said, rising from her chair.

"Then do it. Make that bastard pay for hurting your family."

"OKAY, PATRICK, we'll be live in five, four, three, two, one and—" The light on the camera blinked and Patrick looked directly into the camera. He didn't need any speaking notes or other aids from his communications advisor. He was appearing live on KSEA TV station at the time of day when most of Courage Bay was tuned in. The local news was finished and the station had preempted some programming to give him a chance to talk directly to the city's citizens. Patrick knew exactly what he wanted to say.

He'd explained to the head of the station earlier in the day what he wanted to do, and Timeright Communications, the station's owner, had been more than willing to provide him this public forum. After the day's regular news, Patrick was on a live broadcast to take his message straight to the people. This would be followed by a live phone-in segment with KSEA's news coanchor, Andrew Hayden.

"People of Courage Bay," Patrick began, speaking from his heart to the people he'd seen at yesterday's ribbon-cutting, to the families who'd lost relatives in the crises of the past few months, and to his neighbors, friends and voters.

"For more than one hundred and fifty years, the people of Courage Bay have been known for their selfless and valiant sacrifices in coming to the aid of their fellow citizens in times of disaster. In more recent months, we've seen our own times of crisis. We've lost neighbors, friends and loved ones. We've seen our police officers, our paramedics, firefighters and ambulance drivers risking their lives to avert disaster and save lives. Our hospital staff have worked countless hours of overtime to treat victims of fires, earthquakes, rare viruses, droughts and mud slides.

"Our emergency services teams are stretched to the limits of their endurance. I've repeatedly asked city council for more funding to hire additional emergency personnel and to support the strain on the city's infrastructure and resources.

"As you may be aware, there is a Courage Bay Emergency Fund with several million dollars in it. That fund was set up almost two decades ago to help pay for any unforeseen, extraordinary expenses that might crop up.

"I believe that we need to tap that fund now in order to hire more emergency service workers, keep our emergency equipment in top shape and shorten emergency response times.

"In order to access the emergency fund, we need a one hundred percent yes vote from city council. If you care about your city, your safety and your future, contact your member of city council and demand their support to free up this fund.

"Last night in an emergency meeting, only two of five councilors voted to release much-needed money. It's time for your voices to be heard.

"Your city council was elected by you to serve you, the people of Courage Bay. I urge you to make your feelings known. I'll be standing by for the next hour, taking your phone calls. Please feel free to ask me anything. As your mayor, I'll do my best to answer what I can, and if I don't know the answer, I'll make sure and get it to you within twenty-four hours."

He paused for a sip of water, reminding himself to keep his voice slow and steady. He thought about his mom and about Mrs. Simpson and pretended he was talking to the two of them. By speaking directly to two women he cared for, and who were caretakers themselves, he felt a sense of calm.

"Too much precious time and energy has been wasted. It's time to support your emergency crews. Call now."

The camera switched to Anchorman Hayden, who said, "Thank you, Mayor O'Shea. Our telephone lines are open. The station number is at the bottom of your screen. At the end of the program, we'll also post phone numbers, fax, e-mail and snail mail addresses of all the members of city council. Exercise your right to be heard." Behind the cameraman, the producer held two thumbs up.

"MAYOR'S OFFICE." Briana answered the phone on her desk without glancing away from the television screen in Patrick's office. He was facing the camera, talking sincerely and powerfully, taking his message straight to the people.

As sorry as she was that he'd taken this step without council's knowledge or approval, she couldn't find it in her heart to blame him.

She shifted her attention from the TV screen to listen to her caller. "Is my daddy there?" a young voice asked.

"Is this Dylan?" she asked.

"Yes."

"I'm sorry, Dylan. Your daddy is at the television station right now. He's on TV. If you turn on your set, you'll see him."

"Oh." There was a pause. Then, "When will he be home?"

"Maybe another hour or two. Is everything okay?"

"I guess. I was hoping he'd be home now."

Her heart went out to Dylan. He was obviously upset about something and wanted his dad. Maybe there was something she could do to help, Briana thought.

"Did something go wrong at school today?"

"No."

Well, something must have happened. Had the baby-sitter punished him? Mrs. Simpson had seemed like a decent, caring woman the one time Briana had met her when she brought the kids by to see their dad, but Dylan struck her as a sensitive boy who could be easily hurt. Briana had a feeling that, even though she was younger, Fiona was the tougher one emotionally. Of course, she'd been younger when they lost their mother. Briana was guessing it had hit Dylan hardest.

"Did something happen with Mrs. Simpson?"

While she spoke with Dylan, she kept an eye on the television. Patrick was as appealing on television as he was in person. She had a feeling Dylan would grow up to look similar. Both had the black hair and blue eyes.

"I think maybe it did. She's not here."

Her gaze immediately snapped from the TV screen to the phone as though she could see through it. "What do you mean she's not there?"

"When we were dropped off at home by the car pool, Mrs. Simpson wasn't home and the door was locked. I had to use the secret hidden key." His voice held a touch of pride.

Briana would be smiling at how cute he was if her heart weren't pounding so fast.

"Did the car-pool mom drive away before you and your sister were in the house?"

"Yes."

"Are you alone? You and your sister?" Alarm spiked through her, but she kept it from her tone. They were awfully young to be alone, and she imagined Patrick would have a fit if he knew.

"Yes. I told you. Mrs. Simpson wasn't here when we came in the house. I don't know where she is. She didn't leave a note."

Cursing the woman for abandoning her young charges, Briana grabbed her purse and pulled on her navy linen suit jacket. She could try calling Patrick's mother, or the children's aunt Shannon, but that would only waste time and she suspected she was geographically closest to the children. She couldn't stand to think of those kids alone. "I'm going to come over and sit with you until your dad gets back. Would you like that?"

"I guess."

He tried to sound tough but she heard the relief in his voice.

"I'm leaving the office right now and I should get to your house in about fifteen minutes. Can you do something for me?"

"What?"

"Make sure the doors are locked. Do you remember what I look like?"

"Yes."

"Good. What's Fiona doing right now?"

"She's in the den watching SpongeBob SquarePants."

"That's great. I'll be there as soon as I can. Don't open the door until you know it's me. Okay?"

"Sure."

Normally, Briana wasn't one to speed, but today she couldn't get to Patrick's children fast enough. Her heart pounded and her stomach was in a knot. Maybe she was overreacting, but a nine-year-old and a five-year-old seemed way too young to be on their own. And the poor kid had sounded as if he felt that way, too.

As she neared Patrick's house she noted that some of the stoplights were out, so she was forced to slow down and take the intersections with care. Finally, after what seemed like an hour and was in fact twelve minutes, she pulled up in front of Patrick's house.

She went to the front door, figuring Dylan would be on the watch for her and would already have spied her through a window. She knocked.

"Who is it?"

Smart kid.

"It's Briana Bliss."

The door opened. Her first instinct was to hug Dylan, but she squelched it. He wasn't hers to hug, and she suspected nine-year-old boys weren't big on hugs.

They locked the door behind them and he took her into the den, where his sister was watching a sitcom rerun that didn't look very age appropriate.

"Hey, do you guys want to watch your dad on TV?"

CHAPTER EIGHT

PATRICK WHISTLED as he drove home. He wasn't normally a big one for whistling, but the occasion seemed to demand it. The phone-in TV program had been a bigger success than he'd dreamed possible. It seemed that almost every citizen of Courage Bay had called. The phone lines had stayed jammed and the station had to end the broadcast without having a chance to hear from everyone with something to say.

Regular citizens had phoned in, guys who pumped gas and packed groceries, teachers from the local schools, a cook from the Courage Bay Bar and Grill, homemakers and office workers, retail clerks and business owners. More than ninety percent had supported him in his plea to get that money released. There were some sad phone calls and some downright tragic ones, including a distraught call from Lee Harper, whose wife, Francine, had been killed in the convenience store collapse.

People who'd lost loved ones phoned to plead for the money so others might be saved in the future. Four firefighters called in, some nurses, a doctor or two, an ambulance driver.

The two councilmen who had supported him in last night's meeting both phoned in to make their positions clear.

Councilman Cecil Thomson didn't call and neither did his two cronies. Patrick didn't believe for a second that they hadn't sat glued to their TVs as they faced public humiliation. He was sorry the funding crisis couldn't have been resolved in a less public way, but damn, he was glad to be finally getting somewhere. The message to the three holdout councilmen from their constituents had been loud and clear: Release the money or face a citizens' uproar.

So Patrick whistled. He had the windows open in the car, and he sure hoped no one could hear him, since his whistling was totally off-key—but he had to do something to celebrate.

He pulled in to his garage and cut the engine. He didn't cut the whistling, though. He kept that up as he entered the house, pleased to note that he hadn't missed a chance to see the kids before they went to bed. In fact, if Mrs. Simpson had been watching him on TV with the kids, he probably hadn't even missed dinner.

SURE ENOUGH, something smelled good when he walked in. His mouth watered. It didn't smell a lot like Mrs. Simpson's usual cooking, which tended to include a lot of casseroles that relied heavily on cans of soup tossed over some kind of meat with crushed potato chips on top.

He wondered if she'd been watching one of those cooking shows on TV. There was a definite gourmet odor to his kitchen. The table was neatly set with three places, as per usual, but instead of the regular vinyl table mats, she'd used the good ones from the dining room. That was weird. Was there some special occasion today he'd forgotten about?

Patrick stood stock still for a moment while he ran through all the special days he could think of. His first panicked thought that he'd forgotten one of the kids' birthdays was soon gone. Dylan would turn ten, but not for a couple of weeks yet. They'd already talked about taking some of his buddies to a batting cage and then returning to the house for a family barbecue.

Fiona was a summer baby, and wouldn't be six for several months yet. Mrs. Simpson wasn't big on celebrating her own birthday, but he always gave her a nice check with a card in October.

Stumped, he continued down the hall to the den. "I'm home!" he called out.

"Hi, Daddy!" Fiona shrieked and came flying out of the den in her favorite pink OshKosh corduroy pants and the purple shirt with pink stars on it. Her hair sported little plastic star barrettes. "Hi, Fiona," he said, holding out his arms as she barreled down the hallway for a hug. He swung her up in the air, and she said, "Guess what?" Her eyes were dancing and her chubby little face was pink with excitement.

Before he could attempt a guess, Dylan called to him, "We're in here, Dad." His son sounded so serious, almost as though he were acting the grown-up. Patrick was intrigued. Something was definitely up.

But nothing could have prepared him for the surprise that greeted him when he got to the doorway of the den and saw Briana sitting on the floor, obviously in the middle of a game of Junior Monopoly with the kids. "Surprise," she said softly.

"Is it ever," he admitted, feeling too stunned to consider how he felt about seeing her here in his home, with his kids. "Where's Mrs. Simpson?"

"She had a car accident," Dylan said, his eyes round.

Briana rose, a slight blush coloring her cheeks. "That's right. One of the nurses phoned a little while ago. Mrs. Simpson's in the hospital. Some of the stoplights are out in the area."

He nodded. "I think it's more damage from the aftershock."

"Well, she was driving through the intersection on her way here and someone hit her car. She was knocked unconscious and taken to hospital. She woke up, more worried about the children being alone than about her own health, and couldn't rest until a nurse phoned to make sure there was someone here with the children."

"But how did you know they were alone?"

Briana smiled at Dylan and he almost saw his son's chest puff with pride. "Dylan phoned me at work and explained the situation. We decided it would be a good idea for me to come over."

"Good work, Dylan."

"Anyway," she said, rising from the floor, "Dinner's in the oven. Oh, and it looks like you're going to have to find another sitter for the next couple of days. Mrs. Simpson bruised her ribs in that accident and she has a slight concussion."

He nodded, feeling thick and off center. Briana didn't live in this part of his world, she lived in the work part, and yet in the past forty-eight hours she'd definitely spilled over into his personal life.

The scary part was how much he liked having her there. As dangerous as it was, he let himself imagine, just for a second, what it would be like to have Briana in his life permanently. In two months of working together, they'd discovered a lot of common interests. They both liked traveling and hadn't done nearly enough of it. They both liked *The West Wing,* but also never missed *The Simpsons.* They both liked the outdoors, and although she was a little vague about her family, he sensed they shared a strong attachment to their loved ones.

Briana was a little more organized than he was, and his math was better than hers. They were a good team at work. A fantastic fit physically.

He could so easily imagine what it would be like to walk into the house and find her in casual clothes, the fantastic smell of her cooking wafting through the house. A special expression in her eyes that she saved for him alone.

Sure, he was getting ahead of himself, but at nearly forty years old, he knew when his feelings for a woman were serious.

If she hadn't taken to his kids, he wouldn't indulge such a fantasy even for a moment, but what amazed him was the way she'd acted on Dylan's phone call almost like a mother. She hadn't messed around or tried to find someone else. She'd dropped everything and sped over to sit with his children.

"I don't know what would have happened if you hadn't been there today," he said at last. "Thank you."

He took a step forward, and she took a step forward, and then they realized at the same moment what they were doing and stopped.

"Well," she said, "I should get going now you're home."

"No," both kids cried at once. "We have to finish the game."

"Please?" Fiona said, disentangling herself from Patrick's legs and giving him the pleading look that always turned him into mush. "Can we finish the game?"

"Can she stay for supper, Dad?" Dylan piped up, more enthusiastic than Patrick had seen him in a long time.

"Oh, I don't—"

"Can she stay for a sleepover?" Fiona asked loudly, not to be outdone by her older brother.

He bent to ruffle Fiona's curls, giving Briana a moment to recover her composure. He wasn't going to be the one to say no to that one. In fact, he thought Fiona had a fine idea there.

They were saved by Dylan, who told his sister, "Grown-ups don't have sleepovers."

Well, Dylan had pretty much let Briana know he didn't have women sleeping over on a regular basis, so that was good. And he'd saved both adults from having to comment on Fiona's idea.

Patrick glanced up finally to see that Briana's color had subsided from tomato to more of a watermelon tinge. "Stay for supper. You cooked it. We can at least feed you."

"That's okay, really. I love to cook, and since I moved here, I haven't had a lot of opportunity." She shrugged. "I was happy to have free run of a big, fully equipped kitchen."

"I'm not sure how fully equipped this one is anymore. I'm no gourmet, and Mrs. Simpson's recipes aren't exactly cutting edge. Our pantry runs more to chicken noodle soup and Cheerios than cilantro or lemongrass."

Briana laughed. "That's okay. I used some canned stuff and there were lots of spices in the walk-in storage cupboard. Well, I do want to talk to you about the phone-in show." She smiled hugely. "You were great."

Fiona, who'd been waiting impatiently for a pause in the adult conversation, tugged at Briana's skirt. "Can we finish the game now?"

Briana glanced at Patrick, half-laughing, half-shy. "If you're sure you don't mind me staying for dinner..."

"Absolutely sure," he said. "I'll go change while you finish the game and then we'll eat. Sound good?"

He watched as the three of them settled back to Monopoly. Fiona, he noticed, kept shuffling closer to Briana until the two of them were hip to hip. Briana put an arm around the little girl and looked down at her fondly. Dylan stayed in his own spot, but his eyes never left Briana's face. It seemed to Patrick that Dylan was experiencing his first full-blown crush.

"Get in line, son," Patrick muttered to himself as he headed down the hall to his own room.

Since he was hot and sticky from a long day at work and the lights in the studio, he indulged in a quick shower, then pulled on his usual postwork uniform of jeans and a T-shirt. He thought about shaving for a second time today, but he didn't want anyone—especially himself—getting the wrong idea about tonight.

He left his five o'clock shadow, knowing there'd be no after-dinner nooky with a woman who worked for him. Unfortunately.

By the time he made his way back to the den, he saw that his children were cleaning up the game, so quietly and cooperatively, he wondered for a second if some pod-kids had swapped places with his own. Then he realized they were trying to make a good impression on their guest.

He walked on and found Briana in the kitchen, one of

Mrs. Simpson's aprons wrapped twice around her slim waist. She'd taken a casserole dish out of the oven, filling the room with truly heavenly scents.

"That smells fantastic," he said, his stomach beginning to rumble appreciatively.

"Thanks. It's a superquick version of chicken cacciatore. I hope your children will like it." She glanced at him with a worried expression. "I thought I'd serve it over pasta. Kids like pasta, don't they?"

He had a feeling she could serve Dylan and Fiona nothing but leafy dark-green vegetables and liver and they'd be as excited as though they were eating hot dogs and potato chips. "They love pasta. Thanks again for doing this."

He leaned against the counter and watched her competently serve up four plates of food.

As much as he enjoyed the show, he couldn't stop a frown from forming between his eyes. "I'm going to have a talk to the car pool. I can't believe those women drive off before the kids are inside the house."

She nodded. "I thought the same thing myself. But I've never been in a car pool with children, so I don't know what the protocol is."

"The protocol is safety first, or it should be," he answered shortly. "Whoever was driving today didn't even check to see that Mrs. Simpson's car was out front before leaving a nine-year-old and a five-year-old to fend for themselves."

"The kids did really well, though," Briana reminded him. "Dylan was very responsible. When Mrs. Simpson didn't show up, he called you. And he wouldn't let me in the house until I'd identified myself."

Patrick smiled in spite of himself. His son was plenty responsible, thank God.

"It was bad luck that Mrs. Simpson had that car accident," Briana continued. "Things like that don't happen every day."

"Around here it seems like they do. Damn lights."

"I was thinking about that," she said, turning to him, the ladle in her hand. He watched a single drop of rich, red sauce plop to the counter. "Do you think the lights could be related to the aftershock?"

He nodded. "Maybe. The point is, I need a better backup system for the kids."

She turned back to her task, and there was a moment's silence. Finally she said, "I'd be happy to keep a list of alternative caregivers and all their emergency numbers if you like."

He squeezed the countertop behind him to stop himself from going over there and taking her in his arms. "Briana, I can't think of anyone I'd trust more."

"Don't say that," she said, sounding almost guilty.

He took a step toward her, and she ducked her head again, her color mounting. What was that about? Surely she could take a simple compliment. Or maybe because she didn't have kids of her own, she felt that somehow she wasn't to be trusted. "I do, Briana. I trust you."

If anything, she looked even more uncomfortable. He would have called her on it, but he heard the unmistakable sound of four young feet pounding toward the kitchen.

"Wash your hands for supper," he called out, stopping them in midstride. The pounding retreated and both kids headed for the bathroom before reappearing a few minutes later with clean hands. Dylan, he noted, had even brushed his hair.

Dinner that night was the best meal he'd eaten in his own home in ages. It wasn't just the food—though a woman who could whip up anything that tasted this good, and do it so fast, deserved a medal—but the atmosphere. The four of them had fun being silly. Dylan told some juvenile joke he'd heard at school, and Fiona told Briana about something she'd learned on *Sesame Street,* then when it was clear their dinner guest didn't know the entire cast of the show, his daughter happily enlightened her.

Patrick no longer had to hold up the entire adult end of the conversation. He had help.

Not that the kids needed a lot of prompting to talk. They couldn't wait to tell about their days at school.

"How did you do on your biology test?" Patrick asked his son, remembering they were getting the tests back today.

"I got an A," Dylan said with simple pride.

"That's great," he and Briana said in unison.

"I had to draw a picture of my favorite animal in school," Fiona informed them.

"What did you draw?" Briana asked her.

"Dylan," she said.

It was at moments like this, when his eyes met Briana's in shared amusement, that he realized he'd been lonely. Not the all-by-yourself-with-no-one-to-talk-to lonely. He had a full life as a single dad with a busy job. But lonely in a purely adult way. He missed having a woman in his life. Not just for sex, though he sure as hell missed that, but for companionship. Someone with whom he could make plans for the future, delegate chores, worry over the kids. He missed having a wife and he knew his children missed having a mother.

"Dad, it's rude to stare." Dylan's remark brought him back to the present.

"Hmm?" He blinked and realized that he had been staring at Briana, probably with the same lovesick gaze his son had turned on her earlier. "Oh, sorry. I was lost in thought."

"We watched you on TV, Daddy!" Fiona said, breaking the tension and allowing them to rehash the call-in show.

"I think we'll get our funding now," he told Briana with a smile.

"I'm so glad. Congratulations, you've worked tirelessly for that funding."

"You helped a lot, you know."

"Well," Briana said, rising from the table, "the only thing I could find for dessert was chocolate pudding. I hope that's okay."

"Sweet!" Dylan yelled, jumping up immediately to help clear the plates without even being asked.

Fiona had recently started helping also, though it was painful for Patrick to watch her carry her plate to the dishwasher, her tongue between her teeth as she concentrated on not letting her knife and fork slide off the plate.

"What a big help you guys are," Briana said. "Thanks so much."

After they'd had the pudding, Patrick insisted on finishing the dishes and Briana started to make noises about leaving. "Could you stay and read me my bedtime story?" Fiona asked.

"Um, well, I really should—"

"Briana has to go home to her own house, Fi," Patrick

reminded his daughter. Fiona's lower lip began to tremble. Oh, boy. It looked like the entire family had a crush on his admin assistant.

"Well," Briana said, glancing helplessly at him, "I guess I could read you one story." She disappeared down the hall with Fiona.

After he'd done the dishes, checked his phone messages and gone through the mail, Patrick headed down to Fiona's bedroom to find all three of them in there. Dylan had obviously decided to listen to the story rather than read quietly to himself, as he usually did.

Patrick paused in the doorway and watched the trio. His gut tightened. It was a wonderful picture, a great fantasy. Why the hell couldn't it be real? All Briana had to do was take another job, a job he'd find for her, and they could spend as many nights like this as she was willing to spend. She seemed to like his children, she seemed to enjoy his company, and unless he was badly off the mark, she'd enjoyed their intimacy the other night.

What was holding her back from changing jobs?

"The end," she said, and closed the book, returning it to the shelf. She'd glanced up and seen him standing there. "It's time for me to go now," she told the kids.

Fiona held her arms up mutely for a hug. Briana hesitated a moment, then walked over and hugged her, dropping a kiss on her forehead. "Good night, Fiona."

"Night." Fiona rolled over and pulled her favorite stuffed bunny into her arms.

Dylan walked to his own room and Briana followed him. Patrick stepped to his daughter's bedside and dropped his own kiss on her forehead. "Night, sweetheart."

"Night, Daddy. Love you."

He was in time to see Dylan get the same kiss on the forehead that his sister had, and as Patrick passed Briana in the doorway, their bodies brushed. Oh, man, he wanted more than a kiss on the forehead from this woman.

Once he'd said good-night to his son, he walked back to the kitchen. Briana was standing there with her shoes on and her bag in hand. Suddenly, the atmosphere, which had been so easy all evening, turned awkward. "Well," she said, running her fingers back and forth on the strap of her purse, "I'll get going."

He nodded. "I'll walk you out."

The night was warm for March, and the jacarandas for which the neighborhood, Jacaranda Heights, was named were in full bloom, their scent soft and evocative in the warm night air.

"You don't need to walk me to my car."

"I want to. I want to talk to you."

"Oh."

He waited until they were standing by her car. She unlocked the driver's side but he stilled her hand before she opened the door. "Both my kids got a good-night kiss. What about me?"

She shook her head, refusing to look at him.

He struggled to suppress his frustration.

"I don't suppose I could fire you again until tomorrow morning?" he asked.

She smiled and shook her head once more.

"What I'd really like to do is fire you permanently."

That got her to look up at him. Her eyes were a vivid green in the light from the streetlamps. "You've got no reason—"

He pulled her to him and kissed her with all the pent-up feeling and passion he'd been tamping down since the night in the elevator.

She gave a gasp of shock and stiffened for a second, then seemed to melt into him. She kissed him back, as hungrily as he was kissing her, and he knew one thing. She was as crazy for him as he was for her.

Why then wouldn't she help him make things right?

He pulled away at last, panting and shaken. He was appalled at the sharpness of his desire. "That's my reason," he said.

She put the tip of her tongue out and touched her lips as though amazed at what she and Patrick had just done. "I can't leave my job now."

"Why not?"

"It's complicated, Patrick."

"What the hell is so complicated about it? Do you think Max Zirinsky or Dan Egan wouldn't kill to have you on their staffs? Or there are positions at the hospital at a higher level, with a correspondingly higher wage. What's so complicated about that?"

"I like working in municipal government. That's what I trained in."

"Well, there's plenty of politics in policing and hospital administration."

She rubbed her arms as though she were chilled. "I...I made a commitment. I can't break my word."

"Break it. I don't care. Of course, I'll never find an assistant as good as you. I'll survive. But what about this?" He wrapped his hand around the back of her neck and felt her quiver of response, watched her head tip back so he could kiss her. He spoke softly and from his heart. "Do you think this happens every day?"

She shook her head.

"Briana," he said, realizing he had to be honest with her and let her know what he was feeling, "I'm falling in love with you."

She gasped and made a shushing sound, but now that he'd gone this far, he'd give her all of it. "My kids are falling in love with you. Isn't that worth something?"

"L-love?" she asked, as though it were an unfamiliar term.

"I know it's too soon to be talking like this, and maybe things won't work out between us, I don't know. But I'd sure like to give it a try. In three years I haven't met anyone who makes me feel as—I don't know, as alive, I guess, and full of hope about the future as you do. Please, won't you think about it?"

"I *have* been thinking about it. But what we're doing at work is important, too, and I'm egotistical enough to think that I'm making a meaningful contribution at the office."

"I know. You're right. I'll wait...but not too long."

"Things will improve dramatically when the funding comes through from the bond. Why don't we have this conversation again in a month?"

He nodded once, knowing she was right. Talking his assistant into quitting for entirely personal reasons wasn't the best service he could render the people of Courage Bay. "All right, lady. You've got a month. And in four weeks—less, if things calm down at work enough that I can replace you—you and I have a date with a king-size bed."

"If all you want is sex—" she began, but he cut her off.

"You know it isn't. If I only wanted sex, believe me, I

could be having it every night. There are plenty of single women who actually think I'm a pretty good catch. But for some damned reason, the only woman I want, the only woman who's keeping me awake at night, making me take cold showers and generally making my life hell, is you."

"Oh."

"Yes. Oh. I'm not saying it will work out. Maybe it won't. But in the three years since Janie died, I've barely looked at another woman."

She glanced up, startled. "You mean you've never—" She slapped a hand over her mouth. "I'm sorry. What am I saying? That's none of my business."

He removed her hand from her mouth and kissed the palm. "Of course it's your business. We slept together. I think that gives you a right to know about my sex life. And the answer is no. I haven't had sex with anyone since Janie died. Not until you." He brushed a hand over the gold of her hair, which was like a halo in the streetlight, and wished he could take her back inside and show her how much she meant to him.

"I had no idea." She whispered the words, and it almost sounded as though she were close to tears.

"Well, going without sex for three years is not something you plan. But I loved my wife. I missed her for a long time. I still miss her. I guess I always will. And I was so busy with the kids and work that I…I never got around to dating other women. I missed sex of course. I'm still a man." He grinned in the dark. "But until you came along, I never did anything about it."

He had no idea if he'd just made himself sound pathetic or needy, but he didn't much care. He believed in the truth.

He tried to be truthful always, especially with people he cared about. And he cared about Briana. More than he wanted to.

"I see."

"I'll tell you something else. You can go without for a long time and kind of put it out of your mind, but once you find a woman you desire again, once in three years is not enough."

She laughed softly, but she sounded almost nervous. Why was she so skittish now? She'd been so passionate and open when they were trapped together in the elevator.

Maybe Briana was affected by something in her past, just as he was. He decided to find out.

"Okay. I've told you my story. What's yours?"

"There's not much to tell," she said, easing away from him. They ended up side by side, both leaning against her car.

"You left a job as city manager to come and be an admin assistant. I'm guessing you left your former job for a compelling reason. Bad relationship?"

Her hand was still in his, and now it squeezed into a claw against his palm. *Aha.* But Briana didn't admit to a bad relationship. In fact, she shook her head.

"No. I—I just needed a change." She sighed and looked up into the dark sky. "I was engaged, once. But it didn't work out."

"Did you end up with a broken heart?" That could explain her reluctance to get involved with him.

"No. A few broken illusions, perhaps. He was a slick-talking, smooth-moving cattle rancher, and we hit it off right away. Within six months we were engaged. I started planning the wedding, and he grew a little distant. Then I started showing him decorating magazines. I had such ideas for the ranch house. Oh, and the gourmet kitchen I was going to have installed. That house was badly in need of updating, you understand." She laughed at the memory, but she didn't sound bitter. "He'd usually change the subject whenever talk turned to home-decorating, and I thought it was just because he was a man. But then I happened to mention some ideas for a nursery. He didn't merely change the subject on me that time. He changed women."

"You mean that moron dumped you because you wanted to have kids?"

"Oh, don't make a tragedy out of it. I think he dumped me because he'd gotten carried away on a fantasy of the two of us on a never-ending honeymoon. He thought nothing would change except that he'd have me there in his world, and here I was, hauling curtain samples and kids into his dream. We simply weren't a fit."

Patrick would let her decorate his house any way she wanted, he realized. He'd toss out everything, including the kitchen, and start again if that's what she wanted. With a stirring of mingled pain and hope, he realized he'd even go along with the nursery. He loved kids, and he'd be happy to have more.

But after half declaring his love and seeing her back off, he wasn't about to freak her out with an offer to redecorate and set up a nursery.

If he did, she'd probably run from him faster than the ranch boy had run from her.

What he had to do was get the council back in session

quickly, vote to release the funds and get Courage Bay's emergency services fully functioning again.

Then he could go after the woman he loved.

CHAPTER NINE

PATRICK WAS ACTING exactly as her uncle had predicted, Briana realized as she reached home, battling frustrated lust. Her boss was charming her—not seducing her exactly, but making it very clear he wanted to. Sure, the whole "I've been celibate three years since my wife died" could be a line that hooked women like so many gullible trout, but she couldn't believe that.

Oh, she knew she was in trouble. It wasn't just that Patrick had all but declared his love, which was plenty scary, though also wildly exhilarating. No, it was the way she'd caught herself imagining how nice his kitchen counters would look in granite, and that with a little rearranging, the furniture in the den would work so much better.

She crawled into bed, and Patrick's words came back to echo in her head. *You and I have a date with a king-size bed,* he'd told her, with that fiery glint in his eyes that set her skin sizzling. In an elevator, in the dark, he'd been terrific. And if what he told her was true, he'd also been out of practice.

She smiled a cat-in-cream smile as she stretched among the heap of pillows she'd sewed herself. Patrick in a king-size bed, and back in practice, was something to look forward to.

Of course, her bed wasn't a king, but she had a feeling he'd do just fine in a queen-size bed.

Her body warmed at the thought of what the two of them could get up to between these covers, and she recalled that it would be happening in one short month if she took him up on his challenge. Sooner, if she got the evidence she needed to clear Patrick of wrongdoing.

How exactly was she going to do that, she thought as she yawned, wishing Patrick were beside her and that they were free to work out thorny problems like this together. She was tempted to start by talking to the reporter who'd broken the story in the *Sentinel* and trying to get a good look at the photograph they'd run. But of course it was impossible. Asking a nosy reporter a lot of questions was going to rouse his suspicions. There had to be another way.

It was the last thought she had before falling asleep.

When she woke up the next morning, a few minutes before the alarm was due to shrill, the answer was right there.

She'd been doing this since college, going to sleep pondering a problem and waking with the answer.

Yawning, she stretched and popped out of bed, anxious to get on with her plan. Patrick, as mayor, had access to computer files that were denied her. He had his access code written down in the Rolodex on his desk, cleverly hidden under his dentist's phone number. She'd seen him flip to the number one day when he was checking the municipal budget. Since he hadn't gone to the dentist, she was pretty sure that's what the peculiar number and letter sequence was.

She was certain he didn't think she'd clued in, or if he had, he believed he could trust her. She bit her lip at the thought of his trust and how she was betraying him. When she'd first seen the code, she'd thought nothing of it since she'd had no interest in snooping for information that was denied her at her level of clearance.

Now, as soon as her boss was out of the office for a time, she'd log in using his password and search the police files. She had no idea how much information she could access, but she was going to give it a shot.

"Morning," she said cheerfully when Patrick rolled in a few minutes after her. Her computer was already humming, her e-mail box almost full. Patrick's was probably overflowing. There were six messages piled up at her elbow, and a sheaf of faxes sat neatly stacked on the edge of her desk. She picked up both piles of paper and held them out to him.

"There are seventy-six messages here," she told him. "One hundred percent of these citizens support you in making council vote to access the city's bond."

His face relaxed into a smile. "It's going to be a good day."

"And a busy one," she agreed as both lines began to shrill.

"Mayor's office, can you hold please?" she said to one caller, and picked up the next. "Mayor's office."

"I want to talk to Mayor O'Shea."

"Certainly. Who's calling, please?"

"It's Bonita Alvarez. I voted for the mayor and I want to vote for him again to get the money he needs to do his job."

"Certainly, Ms. Alvarez. I'll put you through."

She reached for the second line, and then noticed that Patrick was still standing by her desk. She'd expected him to go through to his own office. She raised her brows in a silent question.

"Dylan sent you this." He handed her a white piece of paper, the kind used in home computers, rolled into a scroll and fastened with an elastic band, before heading in to his office.

Briana put the second caller on hold until Patrick could deal with Ms. Alvarez, then she pulled the elastic band off the scroll.

Dylan had drawn a picture of a dragon soaring over a castle where some kind of battle was taking place. She guessed Dylan was a kid who'd probably seen *Lord of the Rings* a few times and now lived part-time in a Tolkien universe. Under the picture was a note.

Thanks for the dinner. It was delicious. I hope you can come to our house again sometime.

It was signed simply, *Dylan*. Then, in smaller letters, obviously by the same hand, an addition had been made. *And Fiona.*

Briana loved her picture, and was certain it added a certain something to her decor when she pinned it to her bulletin board. She'd love to take Dylan up on his offer to visit, more than he could possibly imagine. But she had to figure out what his father had been up to first.

She put the second caller through and checked Patrick's schedule. There was a luncheon speech at the CB Business Association, and then at three o'clock he had a meeting with Max Zirinsky. Okay, so she had two opportunities today. She rather thought lunchtime might be her best chance. Whenever she was out at the same time as the mayor, she locked the outer office.

Once that door was locked, it was unlikely anyone would clue in that she was still inside. Snooping on her employer.

The pang of guilt that hit her was almost painful, especially with Dylan's picture hanging on the wall behind her, a constant reminder that if she hurt Patrick, she also hurt his children.

But whoever had hurt Uncle Cecil hadn't worried about *his* family, she reminded herself.

No. As much as she hated to do it, she was going to have to sneak into files she had no business seeing.

There was no time for more soul-searching as the phone rang again. In a sort of counterpoint, the fax machine whirred with astonishing regularity, and the e-mails continued to pour in.

A small percentage of people thought that Patrick was a hothead and a troublemaker. But more than ninety percent of those who responded to his television appeal were offering their support.

Around ten-thirty there was a lull in the phone calls and Patrick came out of his office, stretching his arms.

"Briana," he said, "I think we're going to get the money we need to start serving this community properly."

She smiled dutifully. In truth, she was delighted that the emergency forces were getting the funding they needed, but she also knew this was another blow politically and professionally to her uncle.

If there was anything she could do to help Uncle Cecil save face, she'd do it. He'd been so hurt when she'd tried to talk to him the other night, and still so angry.

"Do you think it would be worth calling Councilman Thomson and the other two who sided with them? Perhaps they'd be more willing to listen to your appeal now they know you have so much public support."

"Oh, they'll listen, all right," he said with relish. "But I'm done crawling to them. Those three can come to me with their hats in their hand."

So much for the olive branch.

They had no time to discuss the matter further because the phone started ringing again. With a comical expression of dismay, Patrick retreated back to his desk.

Briana worked steadily through the rest of the morning. By eleven forty-five, things were quieting down again and she was able to stand up for a stretch herself. Her neck was tight, her shoulders knotted. She'd like to think it was from a morning on the phone, but really, she suspected a lot of her tension was from the knowledge that she was about to spy on her boss.

Well, she comforted herself, he need never know anything about it.

Picking up his speech, she walked into his office. Patrick was already shrugging into his jacket.

"Have you got my speaking notes for this thing?" he asked her.

"Yes. Right here. Archie sent them up earlier."

"Good."

"You'll probably have some questions thrown at you about the funding crisis."

He nodded. Obviously, he'd thought of that, too.

"And I got a call from the *Sentinel*, checking on the time you'd be speaking. I imagine they'll want an update on the results of your call-in show."

"I wouldn't be surprised if all the media were there."

She handed him another sheet. "I prepared these, just in case you need them." As he glanced down at it, she explained, "I've totaled the numbers of calls, e-mails and faxes, and tallied the numbers of those who expressed support and those who were against you. The numbers and percentages are at the bottom. It's not a hundred percent accurate, of course, but it's pretty close. Do you want me to run off a couple of extra copies for any media reps that show up?"

He grinned. "Briana, you are one in a million."

She tried to keep her expression pleasantly neutral, but she had to admit, the compliment thrilled her more than she liked to admit.

But this was the kind of work she loved. Sure, she was overqualified for photocopying and transcribing notes, but she was also helping Patrick with political strategy, which she thrived on. Her salary might be at a clerical level, but the actual work she was doing was challenging.

What could be more rewarding than helping to save a city she'd grown to love?

AFTER MAKING SURE the hallway outside her office was empty, Briana stepped back inside and locked her door. She felt like an intruder. If Patrick returned for something, or the building superintendent needed to get in…well, she'd have a heck of a time explaining what she was doing at her boss's desk, and with the outer door locked.

No help for it. If she was going to be a snoop, she was going to have to get used to the guilt.

She crossed to Patrick's office and took a seat at his desk. Janie smiled at her from the framed photo. There were smaller pictures of Dylan and Fiona, taken at school, Briana imagined. Their innocent faces grinned at her, with that mouthwatering O'Shea grin. Their innocence made her feel small and sneaky and she had to resist the impulse to turn the photos facedown so they wouldn't watch her do her dirty work.

Honestly, she'd never make it in a life of crime.

Flipping through Patrick's Rolodex, she found the card for his dentist. And there was the code, scribbled under the dentist's phone number.

Please, don't let Patrick have changed his access code, she thought as she pulled up the police department's internal Web site. She typed in Patrick's name and his user code, which she'd used often enough. So far, so good.

It took her a few false starts, but she finally got to an area of old arrest files.

Obviously, these weren't used often, so they'd been archived. When she clicked on the file, it asked for her password, and she began to type in the access code on the dentist's file.

Briana got four of the ten digits entered when the phone rang. She was so tense that she jumped a mile and almost screamed. The phone would automatically be routed to the main reception desk at city hall, so she ignored the ringing and took a shaky breath.

Her fingers had hit a wrong key when she'd jumped, so she deleted what she'd typed and reentered the password. She swallowed. There was a risk that this transaction was being monitored somewhere, and that it could come back to Patrick as part of a report, though she'd never seen it happen yet. Still, if the password was outdated and someone noticed...

Well, Patrick had talked often enough about firing her. This would give him cause. She pushed the Enter key.

The file opened.

Since she had both her uncle's name and that of the woman, it didn't take more than five minutes for the particulars of the case to come up. The arresting officer was Joseph Z. Carlton.

Briana felt queasy at the thought of what her aunt and uncle had been subjected to over this. The incident had occurred more than twenty years ago. According to the scant details, which included a file number that probably corresponded to a moth-eaten manila folder filed in an old archive box somewhere, the charges were later dropped.

Or had there ever been any charges in the first place?

Did Joseph Z. Carlton even exist?

Briana knew how close Patrick and Max were. The police chief had been one of Patrick's major supporters. But would either of them have stooped to anything so low as falsifying a police record in order to win a municipal election?

It seemed inconceivable to Briana, but obviously her uncle believed the two men had conspired against him.

She noted all the details, then logged out and carefully returned Patrick's Rolodex to its original position. Grabbing her purse, she left the office, this time for real.

As bad luck would have it, she bumped into Lorna Sinke in the hallway.

"Oh, Briana," the older woman said, looking puzzled. "I thought you'd gone for lunch."

"I forgot something and had to come back," she said, striving for a calm tone. "Is there something you need?"

"No. That's fine. It'll keep."

Briana left the building, knowing she had the first piece of the puzzle—the name of the arresting officer and the police file number. She wanted to know what was in that arrest file and needed to see the original photo.

Once she was in her car, she headed for a mall and found a public pay phone. After calling the police administration office, she asked to speak to Officer Carlton."

"Officer Carson? Susan Carson?"

"No. Carlton. Officer Joseph Z. Carlton."

"There's no officer with that name here, ma'am. What's it regarding?"

She'd had a few minutes on her drive over to come up with a plausible explanation to that very question.

"I'm doing some research on policing methods in the nineteen-eighties," she replied, hoping her voice sounded young. "I'm taking criminology in college, and this is my research project. I went through some old newspaper archives and found Officer Carlton's name in several articles."

"Oh, well, if it was in the eighties, he might have moved on or retired. We've got some officers here who've been on the beat a good long time, though. Want me to put you through to one of them?"

"Okay. Thank you." She decided to wing it and hoped to hell that whoever answered had never spoken to the mayor's administrative assistant.

A click sounded and a few minutes passed. She was starting to lose her nerve and considered hanging up when a gruff voice said, "Brady."

"Officer Brady? I'm a university student..."

She asked Officer Brady a few perfectly useless questions about policing in the eighties, then inquired about the police archives. Although the archives weren't open to the public, she would be able to obtain the name, description and occupation of the persons arrested.

"What if the information has previously been released?" Briana asked. "Like a mug shot." She thought of the celebrity mug shots she saw far too often in the papers and on TV.

"Once it's been released, then that information would be considered in the public domain," the policeman told her.

Briana took a deep breath. "I'm interested in a story that was covered in the *Sentinel* about Councilor Cecil Thomson. A photo taken during the arrest was printed in the paper. I'd like access to that photo."

"Sure," Officer Brady said. "I remember that being in the paper. It caused a scandal at the time. I have to get permission before you can see the picture. Give me your number."

"I'm on the road and don't have a cell phone," she said. "Could I call you back later?"

"Sure. Call around four o'clock. I'll see what I can do."

"Thank you. Um, the arresting officer was Joseph Z. Carlton."

"Joe Carlton. Sure. I remember him. He's been off the force a couple years. He retired to Acadia Springs."

"Thank you very much for your time, Officer Brady."

"Anytime. I'll talk to you later."

Her stomach felt a little jumpy, so she picked up a deli sandwich, which she didn't really want, and forced herself to eat it before returning to the office.

At two forty-five, Briana received a phone call from Patrick telling her that he was on his way to Max's. At the sound of his voice, her heart picked up speed.

"Did the media show?" she asked.

"Yep. I gave them your numbers, and a few sound bites Archie dreamed up. Is the phone still ringing?"

"More phone calls, more faxes, more e-mails. About the same ratio of pro and con."

"Fantastic. No sign of Thomson waving the white flag?"

"Not yet."

"All right. I'll be a while with Max." He paused. "Sure you don't want me to put in a good word for you?"

She smiled wistfully. "You gave me a month," she reminded him.

"Yeah? I don't know who's the bigger idiot. Me or you."

She didn't know either, but she sure hoped it was her.

"I'm not sure if I'll make it back before the end of the day. I'll call you."

"Okay."

At four o'clock, Briana left the building and found a pay phone. If the photo was public property, then she was going to find a way to see it. If it wasn't, she'd have to go to plan B and talk to Officer Carlton himself.

She had no trouble getting through to Officer Brady and he was as helpful as before. "There's no photograph in the arrest file," he told her.

"But...but that's impossible. It was printed in the paper."

"Yeah. I know."

"But..." Her head was whirling. "Could the paper have forgotten to return it?"

"I don't think the picture in the paper came from here."

"But where...?"

"Sorry, honey. I shouldn't tell you this much. Why don't you ask the reporter who printed the story?"

"But he could have made the whole thing up!"

"No. Here's what I can tell you." And he furnished her with the details she'd already found in the police database. Officer Brady offered one extra piece of information, which she'd already read in the paper. Cecil Thomson was arrested for lewd conduct in a public place.

Something was wrong here. Very wrong.

She walked back to her office with a heavy heart, but it was considerably lightened when she received another call from an O'Shea male.

"Briana?" a young voice asked when she answered the phone.

"Yes."

"It's Dylan O'Shea."

"Hello, Dylan." She smiled and glanced at the flying dragon. "Thank you for the picture and your nice note. I have it hanging on my wall so I can see it whenever I turn around."

"Oh. Good. I'm glad you like it."

"I do. Are you looking for your father? He's in a meeting right now with the police chief."

"Oh. No. I was kind of calling to talk to you."

Panic immediately filled her. She was half out of her chair as she said, "Are you alone again? Did something happen?"

"No. We're fine. Mrs. Simpson's still sick, and Grandma couldn't come today, so Dad got this other lady just for today." Dylan dropped his voice. "We don't like her so much. She's kind of grumpy."

"Oh, I'm sorry to hear that. But you know it's only for today."

"Yeah. I guess." He didn't sound thrilled.

"How's Fiona?"

"She's fine. She's watching cartoons."

"Oh. What's the baby-sitter doing?"

"She's watching cartoons, too. They're baby cartoons."

She smiled into the phone, picturing him in his room, bored. "Oh, dear. And you don't have anything to do."

"Yeah. I guess. I can't have a friend over, because this sitter's new. I can't watch a video because of the cartoons. I can't make a noise, even."

"Well, why don't you draw another picture? Your pictures are beautiful."

"What should I draw?" He sounded bored and lonely and she felt for him with all her heart.

"Why don't you draw a get-well picture for Mrs. Simpson? I bet she'd love to have it while she's at home recovering. She'd be happy to know you miss her."

"I don't really miss her that much. But I guess I could draw her a picture. Dad says he's sending her some flowers. He can take the picture over."

"I'm sure she'd like that."

"Yeah. I guess. Well, it was nice talking to you."

Such manners. She had a feeling there was going to be another politician in the family. "It was nice talking to you, too, Dylan."

"Bye."

"Goodbye."

When she got home that night, she went straight to her own computer and pulled up an Internet mapping site. Acadia Springs was disappointingly far away. A three-hour drive, according to her Internet map. It would be a pretty drive—a couple of hours north up the coast and then an hour inland. She confirmed through online white pages that a Joseph Z. Carlton lived there, but decided not to call ahead first. She wanted to surprise the man with a personal visit—judge his reaction to her questions.

She'd drive up there this weekend.

Almost the minute she'd made the decision, the phone rang again. "Mayor's office," she answered, forgetting she was at home. "Hello?"

"It's your uncle Cecil." But it didn't sound like her uncle. There was anger, frustration and a coldness in his voice that he'd never used with her before.

Briana fought down a pang of guilt. It wasn't her fault that Patrick had gone to the people. Although she supported his stand, she hadn't encouraged him to take it. In fact, she hadn't known what he was planning until the day of the broadcast. But still, because she did support Patrick's position, she felt guilty. Her uncle clearly held her in some way culpable.

"What can I do for you, Uncle Cecil?" she said in a conciliatory tone.

"Come on out to our place for lunch on Saturday," he said.

"Saturday?" She'd intended to go up to Acadia Springs on Saturday, but she'd decided not to tell Uncle Cecil about her plans until she'd interviewed Officer Carlton and had all the facts. Now she'd have to go Sunday.

"Yes. Come for lunch. O'Shea's playing hardball. It's time for our team to start playing to win also. I want a full report on how you're doing, young lady. I want him publicly humiliated—he's got to drop this nonsense."

Briana felt herself bristle on Patrick's behalf and her own. She was over thirty, surely beyond being termed a young lady. However, she knew her uncle was clearly upset, so she didn't call him on it. The best thing she could do was go over on the weekend and try and convince him that the wisest course of action would be to acquiesce to the wishes of the people with what grace he could muster.

"Are you getting calls from constituents?" she asked.

"The phone's ringing off the damn hook," he said, and then added some very unflattering things about her boss before hanging up.

The battle lines had obviously been drawn, and neither man was willing to make a conciliatory move.

PATRICK WAS obviously confused and disappointed the following morning that the three councilmen who'd opposed him wouldn't change their positions. He began to talk about putting together a plebiscite.

"The trouble is that a plebiscite takes time to set up and will cost money—money we desperately need to go to our emergency services," he said, pacing her office in frustration.

"Do you want me to set up another emergency council meeting?"

He shook his head. "No point. If those three were planning to change their minds and vote to free up that money, they'd have contacted me by now. No," he said heavily. "I think we're on our own."

"I thought they'd have called by now," she admitted. "They must be receiving almost as many calls as we are."

"Damn that Cecil Thomson. How can he not see that this isn't about petty politics anymore? People are dying unnecessarily because we can't get to them in time. We need more police, more firefighters on call. More manpower, more resources." He sighed and rubbed the back of his neck. "More money."

Briana had listened to Uncle Cecil's advice many times during her career. Maybe it was time he listened to some of hers.

"Patrick, don't start the plebiscite quite yet." She hesitated, searching for a plausible reason not to. "Let's wait one more council meeting. I bet you the gallery will be packed with people demanding answers. Council will be shamed into backing you."

One thing she could say for Patrick was that he did listen to her. He didn't always follow her recommendations, but he did listen and she knew he respected her opinions. This time, he nodded. "You're right as always, Ms. Bliss. Let's give the three holdouts one last chance. But under the terms of the bond, if we can't get council to agree unanimously, a plebiscite can be called. One way or another, we are going to get that money."

CHAPTER TEN

NOON SATURDAY found Briana in a whispered conversation with her aunt while they waited for Uncle Cecil to finish a call in his study.

"Your poor uncle," Aunt Irene whispered. "I'm seriously worried about him. Goodness knows what this fight he's in with the mayor will do to his blood pressure." She shot a glance over at Briana. "And his cholesterol."

Briana could well understand that stress affected blood pressure, but cholesterol?

"He's not sleeping well, and I hear him muttering to himself all the time. It's not right. That mayor had no right to upset your uncle this way."

Briana was about to explain the mayor's rationale, when she realized she'd only upset her aunt further. Briana suspected Uncle Cecil was not a fun man to live with when he was in a temper.

So she held her peace and let her aunt rant on about how dreadful her life had been when that awful photo was first leaked to the press. She couldn't even face going to the supermarket for days. "It wasn't until we were almost completely out of supplies that I realized I was going to have to face the ridicule of our neighbors or starve."

"I'm sorry, Aunt." And she was. "It can't have been easy."

"No. It was terrible. Just terrible." Her lip quivered. "Of course it was a lie. Your uncle has barely looked at another woman since we've been married. He'd never do a thing like...what was in that picture. They'd blanked out part of it, of course, to put it in the newspaper, but it was still just awful. And the man didn't even look like your uncle."

"I'm so sorry, Aunt Irene. I can't believe anyone could hurt you and Uncle Cecil this way."

Still, she wanted proof that Patrick was behind the awful smear campaign.

Interestingly enough, that was exactly what was on her uncle's mind when he emerged from his study.

"You two go out on the back porch and have a nice chat," her aunt said. "I've got the chicken salad all made. I'll just fix the rest of lunch and put it out on the dining room table." She smiled at Briana and added a conspirator's wink. "It's very private out back. No one will see or hear you talking to your uncle."

Briana went through the kitchen and out to the porch. When they were sitting, glasses of lemonade in their hands, she took a moment to study Uncle Cecil. She could see why her aunt was worried about his health. His face was a mottled red, and it wasn't from exertion or too much sun. She suspected it was from high blood pressure and stress.

"Are you all right, Uncle Cecil?" she asked softly.

"Of course I'm not all right." He managed to smile at her. "I'm better for seeing you, though."

She shifted in one of the deck chairs her aunt had reupholstered recently in white cotton with strawberries printed all over it. The print was cheerful, even if the atmosphere was anything but.

Uncle Cecil didn't waste time getting to the point. "Well? What's O'Shea up to?"

Briana felt tugged by loyalty to two men she cared for deeply. If they pulled much harder, she was going to split in two. "You know what he's up to as well as I do, Uncle Cecil. He's determined to access that money, and more than ninety percent of the city's voters agree with him."

Uncle Cecil's cheeks deepened to an alarming hue. He was redder than the berries on the fabric. He put down his drink with a thunk and rose to glare out at his backyard. "He tried to destroy me, and that didn't work. Now he's trying to make a public fool out of me. But he's not going to get away with it."

"Uncle Cecil," she said, in as calm and reasonable a manner as she could manage, "if the people of Courage Bay want to increase funding to the services, would it be so wrong for you to let them do it?"

He turned to her, dumbfounded.

She tried a smile. "I know you understand about money and wise investments, and you wouldn't let anyone be foolish with taxpayers' dollars. I've checked the original documents that were filed when the fund was created. You could stipulate that your yes vote is dependent upon only a certain amount being accessed, and you could demand that council appoint outside trustees to ensure the money is spent wisely."

"I cannot believe my own niece is…is consorting with the enemy."

Briana felt her own cheeks redden at the implied insult.

"I'm not against you, Uncle Cecil. I'm on your side, but I'm also seeing how a lot of citizens feel. I think if you continue to stonewall the mayor on this, you'll end up losing."

"Losing again, you mean."

"I appreciate how angry you are at the way your reputation was smeared, but the two things aren't necessarily related," she said. She rose and placed a hand on her uncle's arm.

"This man all but ruined my life and, even worse, the peace and comfort of my wife, *your aunt.*" He emphasized the last two words, and Briana shifted uncomfortably. "He's not a man anyone can trust. Now, you can't tell me that a beautiful woman like you has been working with him day after day, just the two of you alone in that office, and nothing's happened?"

Knowing that her expression would only too clearly reveal her feelings for Patrick, Briana turned away from her uncle and walked to the other side of the porch.

"He's done nothing improper," she said, reminding herself that she was the one who'd begged Patrick to take her in the elevator, the one who'd talked him into firing her. Now, instead of trying to get her into bed, he'd given her a month to make up her mind about finding another job before he'd continue their private relationship. In her books, that was pretty honorable behavior.

"Maybe you're not trying hard enough," her uncle said from behind her.

She did turn now, knowing her eyes flashed with anger. "I promised you that I would help put things right, and I'm trying to do that and still keep my integrity."

Her uncle shifted uncomfortably, then stooped to one of

the white planters to snap a dead geranium bloom off its bright green stem. "Of course not," he muttered. "You misunderstood me. I'm only trying to right a wrong. If we can turn the city against Mayor O'Shea, then his little publicity stunt to get the money for his old buddies at the firehouse isn't going to work."

"But, Uncle Cecil, this is not a personal whim on the mayor's part. The people of Courage Bay want improved emergency response times. Lives are at stake. People are overwhelmingly in favor of accessing the municipal bond."

"Don't be naive, Briana. You've been involved in politics long enough to know people can change their minds awfully damn fast. If O'Shea were out and I was mayor, I'd run this city more efficiently, and his old buddies Egan and Zirinsky wouldn't get their overpadded budgets past me. I'm an old hand at this and I've been a banker all my life. I think I know a little more about public finance than a man who's spent most of his career sliding down a fire pole!"

"But what if he's right, Uncle Cecil? What if more people die in this town because we don't have the resources to prevent it. How would you feel?"

He looked at her, his blue eyes sharp with suspicion. "I'm beginning to think it's not my feelings that are the problem, but yours."

This time Briana was powerless to stop the heat that flooded her cheeks.

"O'Shea's a handsome young fellow, I'll give you that. Quite a lady's man. All the O'Shea men are. But don't let that Irish charm fool you. He's a coldhearted son of a bitch, out for what he can get, and he'll destroy anyone who gets in his way. I asked for your help because I thought I could trust you. Now I'm beginning to feel the same about you."

"That's funny," she said. "I'm beginning to feel the same way about you."

AFTER SATURDAY'S awkward lunch, where she and her uncle tried to be pleasant to each other for her aunt's sake, Briana was looking forward to a long Sunday drive on her own.

She'd promised she'd help her uncle restore his good reputation. He wanted to do that by bringing down his rival. She much preferred finding out who'd maligned her uncle in that vicious newspaper report. Today, she hoped to get a step closer.

As she drove up the highway, she tossed around ideas on how to approach the retired officer. In the end, she decided to tell as much of the truth as she could. She'd be up front about the fact that she worked for the mayor and would explain that she was researching the old charges in hopes of exonerating the long serving councilor. With time running out before a showdown between Patrick and Cecil Thomson, Briana was determined to get to the truth.

When she reached the tidy community of small bungalows, she found the Carlton home with no trouble. As she pulled to the curb, she noted that all the drapes were drawn and the newspaper sitting on the front step.

Maybe they were out for the afternoon?

She got out of her car and headed up the path, but as she rang the front doorbell and listened to it echo, a voice said behind her, "They're not home."

Briana turned to find an older woman in a sun visor,

plaid shorts and a short-sleeved T-shirt regarding her with mild suspicion.

"Oh. I drove up from Courage Bay to see Mr. Carlton on business. Will he be home this afternoon, do you think?"

"Nope. Not till the middle of the week. They're on a cruise for their fiftieth wedding anniversary. You want to leave a note?"

Briana smiled and shook her head. "I was hoping to talk to him in person. But it can wait. Thank you for your trouble."

"It's no trouble. We look out for each other in this neighborhood."

MONDAY MORNING, Patrick handed Briana a small envelope.

"What's this?" she asked.

"It's from Dylan."

She wasn't surprised. Dylan now contacted her every day, either by phone or by sending her a new piece of art for her bulletin board. She was falling for him almost as badly as she had fallen for his dad.

Inside the envelope was a single card with space aliens on it and several lines printed in Dylan's own hand. It took her a moment to realize what it was. "Oh, a birthday party invitation."

"That's right. Dylan wanted to invite you to his party."

She glanced up at Patrick. They'd been so careful this past week to keep their distance, and though she couldn't bring herself to discourage Dylan's calls, she hadn't made another trip to the O'Shea house. She hadn't intended to until she knew the truth about the false charges against her uncle. She'd been fairly certain Patrick would give her the month he'd promised, but she hadn't counted on his son being the one to invite her back to their home.

"Did you know about this?"

"Sure." Patrick was noncommittal. He could love the idea or hate it—it was impossible to tell. So she asked him.

"How do you feel about this?"

"It's Dylan's birthday party. He can invite anyone he wants."

Okay, he wasn't exactly forthcoming with his feelings. She hesitated, tapping the card against her palm. "I'm flattered that Dylan invited me, but I'm not sure it would send the right message if I—"

"Don't tell me. I didn't invite you. Tell Dylan." Patrick pointed to the last line. "It says RSVP right there." He turned and disappeared into his office.

Briana had the feeling he was disappointed she was going to turn down his son's invitation. But she had to, didn't she?

Later that day, when she called Dylan, he whooped with joy at the sound of her voice, and Briana knew right then that she was going to his party.

"I knew you'd come," Dylan said enthusiastically when she accepted his invitation. I told Dad you would."

"Really." She paused in surprise. "Did he think I wouldn't?"

"He said you had your own life and I shouldn't be disappointed if you couldn't make it. But I would have been."

So, she'd spend Saturday afternoon at the birthday party desperately pretending she didn't have the hots for Dylan's father.

At least she had a good idea what to get Patrick's son

for his birthday and spent a happy hour in an arts and crafts store downtown selecting a drawing kit that was age-appropriate and yet offered him some tools and an instruction book if he wanted to learn more. She also picked up a three-volume set of *The Lord of the Rings*, figuring that no matter how good a movie was, it could never capture all the nuances of the original book.

While she was in the bookstore, she picked up a book for Fiona, as well, knowing that she was young enough to feel left out when Dylan got all the presents.

Since she wasn't in the habit of buying kids birthday gifts, Briana didn't have the right kind of wrapping paper. She found a card shop and bought paper with realistic-looking dinosaurs and a "now you are 10" card.

That was the easy part.

The tough part came Saturday afternoon when she had to decide what a thirty-two-year-old woman should wear to a ten-year-old's birthday party.

"This is ridiculous!" she yelled to herself after she'd changed her outfit more times than a runway model for a Paris show. She finally decided on a denim skirt, leather sandals, a pale blue shirt and a white cotton sweater.

As she drove to the party, she had no idea what to expect. Her big fear was that, for all the supposed casualness of the invitation, she'd be the only adult other than Patrick, which might in some way cast her as the mother figure for the day.

Of course, she'd tried to pump Patrick for details of the party, but, being a man, he didn't seem to catch on to the subtext of her questions the way a woman would.

When she'd asked him, "Has Dylan invited many

boys?" what she really meant was, "Will I be the only woman there?"

Patrick had answered absently, signing a stack of correspondence. "I gave him a limit of ten boys."

"Oh. Was I included in that limit?"

He glanced up, a twinkle of amusement in his eyes. "You're not a boy."

She gave up. She absolutely gave up.

Now, as she drove up to Patrick's house, she was surprised to see a string of cars lining the driveway and parked out front.

When she climbed out of her car, she heard unmistakable sounds of adult merriment. Clearly, then, there were more than just ten boys here at the party. Oh, well, her worst fear was banished. She wasn't being chosen as stand-in mother for the day. Dylan had simply invited her because he wanted her to be there.

Breathing a huge sigh of relief, she walked to the front door and rang the bell. She was about to ring again when a harassed-looking Patrick opened the door. Briana had anticipated feeling a little awkwardness at being in his home again, but he was so clearly frazzled that any nervousness immediately fled in the need to help him in some way.

"Do you know anything about potato salad?" he asked.

It was impossible not to smile. He was adorable when he was flustered. "The basics. Why?"

"I forgot to buy it from the deli. Dylan loves potato salad. He can't turn ten without it and I've got a potful of boiling potatoes on the stove, ten demons from hell destroying my house, guests in the backyard I'm ignoring and no clue what to do first."

So the man could run a city in crisis, but a simple kids' party was beyond him. Briana had no idea why she found that so appealing, but she did.

"I can handle the potato salad," she said, entering the house. She handed him the presents and started pulling off her sweater. "But the ten demons from hell are your department."

He shot her a grateful grin.

"Thanks. I owe you."

Since she knew her way around his kitchen, she went straight in, trying to ignore the howls and yells of the boys currently stampeding through the house. Demons from hell wasn't so far off, she decided.

The potatoes were boiling merrily in the pot. Patrick hadn't peeled them before putting them on to cook, but she could deal with that. She opened the cutlery drawer, found a fork and pushed it into a random potato. Still hard. Good.

"How do you know where Patrick keeps his cutlery?" a sharp voice from the sliding doors leading into the backyard made her jump and almost drop the fork.

Swinging round, she saw Shannon, Patrick's younger sister—you could never call her little—staring at her with an expression that was far from benign.

Why shouldn't she know where Patrick kept his cutlery? There was an innocent enough explanation, but she hadn't seen Shannon since the night she'd helped rescue Patrick and Briana from the elevator, and the same suspicious gaze was riveted on her now.

Briana noticed then that the adults she'd heard out in the yard weren't just parents of the other boys. There were a lot of O'Sheas out on the lawn, laughing and talking. In fact, Briana realized with a stab of panic that the birthday party was as much a family gathering as a kids' affair.

Shannon slid the door closed and came closer.

"Lucky guess," Briana told her. "Patrick's having potato salad angst. Since you're obviously more familiar with his kitchen, why don't you make the salad?" She stepped back and made a graceful gesture toward the pot.

Shannon shrugged and sent her a wry smile. "Potato salad's not my specialty."

"Wash your hands and grab a knife. You can be my sous-chef."

While Shannon did just that, she said, "I'm surprised Patrick invited you."

"Patrick didn't invite me," Briana assured Patrick's nosy sister. "Dylan did."

"Oh. He's a nice kid. More sensitive than he looks."

"I wasn't sure what to wear," Briana said, only half-teasing. "The last time I was at a ten-year-old's birthday party, I think I wore pigtails and a Cabbage Patch doll T-shirt."

This sally didn't receive so much as a smidgen of a grin in return. "Why are you here?"

"I told you, Dylan invited me."

"Yeah. But you didn't have to say yes. You look like a woman who gets a lot of weekend invitations."

Briana understood that Shannon was protective of her brother and her niece and nephew. She respected that, so instead of getting snippy, she was honest. Letting out a breath, she turned to lean against the kitchen counter. "I planned to say no, but it's harder than you'd think to say no to Dylan."

Shannon emitted a surprisingly musical laugh. "Don't I know it. All the O'Shea men inherited the Irish charm."

Briana nodded and turned back to recheck the potatoes. Patrick sure had charm, and it had worked on her all right. She turned off the stove burner.

"You probably think I'm being pushy and sticking my nose in where it doesn't belong," Shannon remarked.

Briana didn't answer.

Behind her, Shannon snorted. "Okay, I am being pushy and sticking my nose in, but I love Patrick and Dylan and Fiona and I don't want to see them hurt."

"Patrick and I aren't—"

"Save it. I've seen the way you look at each other. I'm not stupid." She pushed her hair away from her face. "You didn't know Patrick when Janie was alive."

This got Briana's attention. She turned and gazed at Shannon. "No. I didn't."

Shannon's gaze clouded. "It broke us all up when it happened. Janie wasn't even sick. One day, everything's fine. Patrick's got this perfect life. He's married to the girl he started dating in high school. He's got these two great kids. He's the fire chief. Life can't get any better. And then poof. It's over."

"Tell me about it," Briana suggested gently. It was obvious this was tough on Shannon, but she was the one who'd opened the subject, and Briana really wanted to know more.

The usually tough firefighter rubbed the heel of her hand against her forehead. "Janie woke up that morning and said she wasn't feeling well. She had a headache. So Patrick told her to stay in bed. He got the kids up and gave them their breakfast. Dylan was in first grade. Fiona was only two. Patrick dropped Dylan off at school, and to give Janie a break, he took Fiona to our mom's for a few hours."

Shannon shook her head. "Thank God he did. Janie died that morning. Patrick had run home to check on her and he found her on the floor. She had the phone in her hand. She must have been trying to call for help." Her gaze sharpened on Briana. "You think he's ever forgiven himself for leaving her that morning?"

"But she only said she had a headache." Briana shrugged. "Most people would take a pill and not think anything of it. Why would he worry? I mean, it's a terrible, terrible tragedy, but I don't see how Patrick can blame himself."

Shannon looked at her steadily for a moment. "I'm going to tell you something not very many people know. No one outside the family knows. Janie couldn't take a pain reliever. She was pregnant." She swallowed noisily, and Briana thought that as formidable a foe as Shannon could obviously be, she was also the kind who loved, and deeply. It was clearly painful for her to talk about her sister-in-law's death.

"Oh, no."

"She was only three months along, but Patrick blames himself for that, too. He was the one who wanted more kids. I don't think Janie minded either way, but he'd come from this big loud family, and that's what he wanted. And he ended up losing his wife, as well as the baby she carried."

"But that wasn't his fault!" Briana cried, moved almost to tears by the story.

"Tell him that."

She drained the potatoes and filled the pot with cold

water, letting this new information seep in. "Of course he blames himself. I guess I would in the same situation."

"So maybe now you can see why I won't have him hurt. I'll tell you right now, and it's not to minister to your vanity, but in the three years since Janie's been gone, I've never seen him look at another woman the way he looks at you. And that scares me."

"I don't want to hurt him," Briana said softly. And it was the truth, but not the whole truth. She'd come to Courage Bay to hurt him. To revenge her family. She felt sick inside.

"If you do, if you hurt him or those kids, I promise I will take you apart."

This was not a promise Briana took lightly. One glance at those fierce blue eyes, and she knew she'd never want to cross Patrick's sister.

She nodded. "Thank you for telling me."

"I'm not stupid, you know. He won't tell me anything, but I know you two weren't playing charades inside that elevator. He's got it bad." She shook her head, hair falling around her face. "Besides, you look at him the same way he looks at you."

Briana blinked, startled. She did? She thought her feelings for Patrick were her secret, and here she was broadcasting them every time she looked his way?

Not good.

"Don't worry," Shannon said, relaxing once more. "I don't think anyone but me has noticed." She chuckled. "It was pretty hard not to notice when you came out of that elevator with your blouse hanging open and the pair of you looking like…well, I don't think the earthquake was the only thing that made the earth move."

"This is a very inappropriate conversation," Briana said, trying hard not to blush. Since she knew she was going a deeper red by the second, she stuck her head over the pot and started taking out potatoes. She shoved a couple Shannon's way. "Here. Peel these."

"Ow," her companion said. "They're hot."

"You're a firefighter. You're supposed to be able to take the heat."

"Not in the kitchen," Shannon grumbled. But she dug in and peeled potatoes, hot or not.

The sliding door opened and a huge man entered. The way he and Shannon looked at each other, Briana didn't have to be introduced. Obviously, this was John Forester.

"Now that's a sight for sore eyes—you being domestic," he teased Shannon.

She laughed and introduced John and Briana.

"What are you doing in here?" Shannon asked.

"I'm hungry."

"You're always hungry. The food will be up in a minute. Go help Sean with the barbecue or something."

With some good-natured muttering, John left and the two women went back to their potato salad.

Briana once more found herself raiding Patrick's fridge and pantry for the ingredients she needed. There was lots of mayonnaise in the fridge, luckily, and some gourmet oil and vinegar dressing, which she threw in. No green onions, but she chopped up some celery and carrots. Patrick hadn't boiled any eggs, so she decided to do without them. She got creative with some spices, mixed the whole thing together and found a pretty glass bowl to put the salad into. When she and Shannon were done, they had a very respectable-looking potato salad, and when they tasted it, they both approved.

"At least you're a good cook," Shannon said, helping herself to another scoop of potato salad, before Briana ruthlessly pulled it away and put it in the fridge.

Shannon started to wipe down the counter. "Look, I haven't told many people this yet, but I'm thinking of moving to New York to be with John."

"Wow. The family will miss you."

"I know. Anyhow, I guess that's why I was hard on you. I won't be around to keep an eye on Patrick and the kids, so I have to get my licks in now."

"I understand." And she did. Family loyalty could make a person do some crazy things.

Now that Shannon had leveled with her, she seemed to loosen up around Briana, which was good. The only thing was, she didn't want to be the great hope for Patrick's future any more than she wanted to be the woman who brought him down with a sexual harassment charge.

Briana wanted a chance to get to know this man her body craved, who he really was, without the rest of the world looking on.

In a crowd of O'Sheas, that wasn't likely to happen.

Surprisingly, as it turned out, Briana did get to know more about him that afternoon. She saw him with his family, relaxed in a sunny backyard with the smell of grilling burgers in the air.

They were a gregarious lot, the O'Sheas, and those she didn't know, she soon met. Shannon made sure of it. She dragged Briana by the hand to meet her parents.

"Mom," Shannon said, interrupting the older woman's

conversation, "this is Patrick's new admin assistant, Briana Bliss. Briana, this is our mom, Mary."

Mary O'Shea was as tall as her daughter. She looked about fifty, when Briana knew she had to be at least ten years older. She wasn't a beautiful woman, but she was a striking one, with the most amazing cloud of long, white curly hair that floated around her head and shoulders in a way that was far too angelic for the expression in her twinkling hazel eyes. She looked like a woman who enjoyed a good joke and could keep her crew of men in line with no trouble at all.

"It's a pleasure to meet you," Mary said, and instead of shaking Briana's hand politely, she pulled her in for a rib-crushing hug. "Patrick thinks the world of you, you know. He's lucky to have you."

"Thank you," Briana said faintly, wondering if she'd bruise.

"This is Patrick's father, my husband, Caleb," Mary said, jabbing her husband in the belly with her elbow to get his attention.

Caleb was tall—about six foot five—and probably weighed in about three hundred pounds. Even though he was completely bald, he was a handsome man, with the same gorgeous blue eyes and thick black lashes as Patrick.

Not certain she could survive a hug if he was as enthusiastic as his wife, Briana was relieved when he shook her hand heartily with his own work-roughened hand. "Patrick's lucky to have such a pretty little thing in his office," the older man said with an appreciative spark in his eye.

"You are so politically correct, Dad," Shannon said, rolling her eyes at him.

Caleb only laughed, a big booming laugh. "I know Briana's excellent at her job, because my son told me so. Don't see why me thinking she's pretty is a crime."

Briana was dazed rather than offended. At five feet ten she didn't often get called a "pretty little thing," but the O'Sheas all seemed to dwarf her. She decided she liked Caleb with his humorous gaze and hearty laugh, so she smiled up at him. "I'm not offended. Thank you for the compliment."

Shannon was summoned away by John, so her father took it upon himself to introduce the rest of his clan, which included Brian O'Shea, Patrick's grandfather, Sean O'Shea, Patrick and Shannon's brother, who was a smoke jumper with the fire department, and his wife, Linda.

Even though it was a family party, the O'Sheas put Briana at ease, and she was soon enjoying herself more than she'd imagined she would.

Dylan roared past with a "Hi, Briana," giving her his soon-to-be-chick-magnet grin and racing on to the next game with his crew of equally noisy friends. He seemed delighted to see her, but no more so than he was happy to see everyone else.

Fiona also had a friend over, the younger sister of one of Dylan's pals, and the two little girls were sitting cross-legged on a quilt under a leafy tree, playing dolls. Briana walked over and paused to watch the girls. She couldn't believe the difference between the orderly, low-key girls' play and the rambunctious antics of the older boys.

She didn't want to interrupt Fiona and her friend, but couldn't stop herself from enjoying the scene for a few minutes.

"Sugar and spice and everything nice?" a deep male voice said softly behind her.

Since her body immediately perked to attention, it was obvious who was speaking. She turned to find Patrick altogether too close and looking more relaxed now.

She smiled at him, wishing she had the right to put her arms around him and kiss him. Wishing he didn't look at her in a way that put the idea into her head.

"Will Fiona and her little friend be that noisy when they're Dylan's age?" she asked.

She ought to take a couple of steps back, Briana thought, but her body wouldn't obey the dictates of her more sensible brain. He was so close she could see the black flecks in his eyes, the lines of both laughter and tragedy endured that radiated from the corners of his eyes, the darker patch of stubble on one side of his jaw where he'd missed a spot shaving. She could even smell him, the clean laundry smell of his T-shirt and the earthy and so-familiar scent of his skin. It took her back to the dark elevator, when she'd been surrounded by his scent, the feel of his skin, the sound of his voice.

The pull she felt was like a physical tug.

"I doubt it. I think boys are just rowdier."

And which gender would he have ended up having more of, she wondered, if his wife hadn't died? Boys or girls? It was a sad thought for a sunny day, but the information was so new to her that she needed to digest it. She wished she could ask Patrick, encourage him to open up and talk to her about that awful time. But she didn't have the right. She already felt an intimacy she didn't want to feel, and to encourage it at this point was crazy.

"You look like you're miles away," Patrick said.

"Sorry. I think I'm in shock. I had no idea Dylan and his friends had so much energy."

He chuckled. "He'll sleep tonight. They all will. And I'm sorry I didn't give you much of a welcome. You caught me in the middle of a panic."

She smiled, thinking how much she liked the carefree sound of his laughter, and how rare that laughter was these days. "As I believe I told you, I love to cook."

"The salad looks great. Thanks for helping me out."

"What are friends for?"

"Is that what we are, Briana? Friends?"

Briana had asked the question idly, and his reply stunned her. She blinked and stared at Patrick, so serious and so handsome with the sunlight glinting off his black hair, his blue eyes intent on her.

"I—I'd like to think we are."

He gazed at her as though there was a lot more he wanted to say, and couldn't. He merely nodded, and she noted the tense set of his shoulders as he turned and strolled over to his brother Sean, who was helping John flip burgers.

She didn't see Patrick again until it was time for cake and presents. Since there were no kids in her own life—most of her friends being young, childless professionals—she was ridiculously nervous about her gift for Dylan. Was it too old? Too...artistic? She didn't want to disappoint Dylan with a lame gift, and now she wondered if she'd been wise to include her small present for Fiona.

Oh, well, she'd done it with the best of intentions. Quietly she handed the little girl the wrapped package when

Dylan opened his. Fiona was delighted, and her dainty little fingers made surprisingly short work of the wrapping.

"It's a book!" Fiona showed it to Briana as though it would be a surprise for her, as well. She'd asked at the bookstore and hoped she had something age-appropriate, and the story was about a small black dog who got lost and had to find his way home. It seemed to be a hit with Fiona.

Dylan ripped the wrapping paper off his gift. "Wow. Cool," he said as he opened the case and spied all the art supplies. "Thanks. I'll draw you the first picture." He flashed her that grin again, then opened his book and pumped his fist in the air. "Yes!"

He opened his other gifts, but the biggest excitement was saved for his father's present—a black mountain bike with a glossy black helmet to match.

"Sweet!" Dylan yelled. "Now we can go biking together, Dad."

Briana only hoped life in Courage Bay would calm down enough that the father and son could enjoy plenty of weekend bike rides.

She smiled to herself. While they were doing that, she and Fiona could spend some quality girl time making cookies, doing manicures, decorating the doll's house she'd spied in the little girl's room. Briana was dying to get her hands on it. And when Fiona was a little older, she imagined the four of them out riding together.

Abruptly she yanked her daydreams back to reality. What was she thinking? She never should have come here today and allowed herself to fall into the fantasy that she was part of the O'Shea clan.

Until she'd cleared her uncle's name, she needed to

keep her distance from the O'Sheas—all of them. If by some slim chance Patrick had been a party to hurting her family, the two of them could never have a future together.

Briana forced herself to drink coffee and chat to Mary O'Shea as though she weren't counting the seconds until she could leave.

Then, suddenly, nine of the boisterous young boys were being taken home, and relative quiet descended on Patrick's home. Good. Her moment to escape had arrived.

After a short conversation with Patrick and John, Shannon clapped her hands. "Do the birthday boy and his sister want to come have a sleepover at Auntie Shannon's?"

Over the shrieks of glee and the pleas, "Can you make pancakes in the morning? Can we take Cleo for a walk?" Briana felt her stomach contract.

Damn that interfering, *matchmaking* Shannon O'Shea. Briana had liked her better when she was threatening her than she did now that the woman was trying to foster a relationship between Briana and Patrick that was both inappropriate and fraught with potential heartache.

Briana knew perfectly well that the sleepover was a ploy to give her and Patrick time alone. It had to be the least subtle ploy she'd ever seen, and in front of his whole family, too! Not that anyone seemed to mind. Mary, for one, had a complacent smile on her face, and she saw the older woman reach for her husband's hand and give it a quick squeeze.

Oh, no.

Briana didn't want time alone with Patrick. Well, okay, she did, but not while everything was such a mess, and she was so confused.

No. She couldn't and wouldn't be manipulated like this. As well-meaning as his sister was, Shannon was also, as she'd warned Briana, pushy. For some reason, Patrick's sister had now decided to sanction the romance, but Briana needed to let it be known to every O'Shea in Courage Bay that she made her own decisions. And being offered a night alone with Patrick on a silver platter was more tempting than she liked to admit, but she wasn't ready for that delicacy quite yet.

In the pandemonium of the kids getting ready to go, and before Patrick's family had a chance to leave, she retrieved her coat. Her color was high, she knew, but she couldn't help that. Maybe they'd think she'd caught a touch of sun.

"Thank you for a lovely party," she said to Dylan, who was running around the kitchen with his sleeping bag, shouting something about not needing a toothbrush.

Patrick didn't seem to agree on the toothbrush situation and was down in the bathroom, she presumed, yelling something about cavities.

"Thanks for the present," Dylan said. "I mean, thanks for coming."

"I had a good time. You enjoy your sleepover."

Then she gave Shannon her blandest smile, wished every O'Shea in the vicinity a pleasant evening, and headed out while the O'Shea she most cared about was down the hall in his children's bathroom.

And take that, Shannon, she said to herself as she scooted into her car and drove home.

CHAPTER ELEVEN

BRIANA STARED at the grainy photocopy of the newspaper story and photo that had destroyed her uncle's chance at being mayor and felt a surge of irritation. Uncle Cecil should hire a lawyer and a private investigator and find out once and for all who'd planted the false story and evidence. Her uncle insisted he wouldn't have her aunt hurt, but he didn't seem to consider that this whole mess was hurting his niece.

As much as she wanted to help her uncle, she was putting her own career in jeopardy. She'd come to Courage Bay so angry on her aunt and uncle's behalf that she couldn't see straight, never mind think straight. But she'd had two months to gain some perspective and she'd also discovered that she loved Courage Bay, enough that she wanted to put down some roots and stay awhile. Maybe forever. She could no longer contemplate a political hit-and-run operation.

Once Briana had done as much of the legwork as she could to find the culprit behind this story, she'd insist Uncle Cecil launch a formal investigation or drop his vendetta. That was a more honorable course than trying to destroy Patrick's career.

Even as she tried to focus on the photo, her sneaky mind kept transporting her to that house in Jacaranda Heights, where, even now, Patrick was cleaning up after the party, or maybe doing some quiet activity of his own, since he had the house to himself.

All night long.

Lust grabbed at her with sharp claws and she gritted her teeth to stop herself from driving back over to his place. But maybe once she'd left, Shannon had reneged on the invitation to the kids, and Patrick and his family were all playing one of the new video games Dylan had received for his birthday.

No. Shannon wouldn't back out of her invitation, not when Fiona and Dylan had been so excited. Patrick was on his own all right, unless he'd decided to use his freedom to do some socializing. She didn't like how that thought made her feel, but then she'd had her chance to be the one "socializing" with Patrick, and she'd declined the treat.

But her restlessness didn't abate.

She put the newspaper article down on her kitchen counter. What was she thinking? It was Saturday night. She should have gone out. One of the girls at work was having a party tonight. She could go. But having already turned down a dinner invitation from a man who might now be there, she'd decided to stay home.

Sometimes, being single sucked.

Having decided that, she wandered into the kitchen. She wasn't starving exactly, since she'd had a burger for lunch, but cooking always soothed her. There was a nice bottle of Pinot Gris in the fridge, which she opened. She put Sarah McLachlan on the CD player, took out salad greens and a free-range chicken breast and started cooking.

She was humming, her salad dressing half-made, when there was a knock at her door.

Odd. Everyone she knew would call before coming over. Maybe it was someone canvassing for some cause or a neighbor looking for a lost cat.

She opened the door and Patrick stood on her doorstep, apparently as surprised to be there as she was to see him. And she was far too happy to see him.

"Hi," she said, noting that his eyes were almost navy in the dim evening light.

"Hi." He didn't make a move to come in and didn't seem to have much to say for himself.

Wanting to help him out, she asked, "Did I forget something at Dylan's party?"

"Yes." It must have been her sweater. But he wasn't carrying anything, and then she remembered she'd draped her sweater over a chair in the kitchen.

"Okay. What?"

"You forgot to say goodbye."

"I said goodbye to Dylan. He's the one who invited me."

"Right. But I'm the one who missed you when you left."

"Oh, Patrick. You mustn't say things like that." He was playing right into her uncle's hands and she didn't want him to.

"I know." She opened the door wider and he leaned his shoulder against the jamb. "I don't want to want you this much. I said I'd give you a month, and it hasn't even been two weeks."

She nodded. She could count the days as well as he could. And she had been.

"But I have a problem." He glanced up at her, so solemn, his blue eyes frank and intense. "I'm crazy about you."

Her heart did a perfect somersault. "Oh, Patrick."

"Do you think I could come in for a minute?"

She nodded and let him in. Without bothering to ask if he wanted one, she poured him a glass of wine and led him into her tiny living area, where she took a seat and gestured him into the one opposite her.

He fiddled with the stem of his glass. Sipped. Put the glass down on the rattan coffee table. She was irrationally glad she'd bought some fresh red tulips today and put them in a vase, not that he appeared to notice them.

"We never should have made love," he said almost savagely.

Her mouth opened, but he went on before she could speak.

"No. That's not true. I never should have hired you. I saw your résumé and I knew you were overqualified for the job. If I hadn't hired you, I'd have met you some other way. I've tried so hard to stay away, Briana, but after the night in the elevator, I can't stop thinking about you."

Her heart was pounding at a ridiculous rate. "I… Oh, Patrick."

"Honey, I don't think I can wait a month for you."

"But you promised me—"

"I know I did. I've considered resigning as mayor."

She blinked. He was handing her the answer to all her troubles on a silver platter. If he resigned, then her uncle would have achieved his goal. Maybe Uncle Cecil could have another shot at the job himself. Except that, family loyalty aside, she knew Patrick was doing the right thing for Courage Bay, and now was not the time for change.

"You can't do that!" she cried.

"That's the conclusion I came to also. Please, Briana, I'm asking you as a man in pain, please consider another job."

"But we agreed to wait until after—"

"I know. But you could put in for a transfer and we could post your position. You wouldn't have to leave the mayor's office for a month or so."

What could she do? She was only human, and she knew his need so well because it was the same as her own. Now that he was here, the temptation was too great. "I wish you hadn't come."

"I couldn't stand being in that house all by myself when I knew damn well, just as you did, that Shannon pulled that stunt so we'd have some time together."

"It was pretty high-handed of her. Not to mention inappropriate."

He snorted. "Get used to it. That's my sister."

"Patrick, I…" She what? Didn't want him? Thought her job as an admin assistant was more important than the most promising relationship she'd had in her life?

Maybe it was time for the truth. Part of the truth, anyway. "Until this crisis is resolved, I'm staying." She rose and brought her copy of the grainy newspaper photo and handed it to him. After he'd looked at it, he put the paper down on the table with an expression of distaste.

"What are you doing with that?" he asked.

She wouldn't lie. She'd keep her uncle's role confidential but she wouldn't lie. "I've been doing some research. I think this photo is one of the reasons Cecil Thomson is your enemy on council."

Patrick stared up at her. "It's got nothing to do with me."

She chose her words carefully. "But the article did come out right at a crucial moment in the election campaign. Cecil Thomson was predicted to win easily, and then this article and the photo were published and you won by a landslide."

Patrick was frowning at her. "Are you suggesting I sent that article to the *Sentinel*? What, you thought I had an old photo lying around of Thomson getting a blowjob from a hooker? How could—"

"No. No. Not you. But maybe someone who badly wanted you to win. You have to admit it was unfortunate timing."

"I never liked Cecil Thomson much, but I wouldn't have believed he'd act like that. I've lived in Courage Bay my whole life. You get to know things. There are a lot of things I don't like about Thomson, but he's never been a man you'd figure to have skeletons in his closet. I was as shocked as anyone."

She picked up the photocopy and stared at it. "Are you sure it's real?"

Patrick's eyes widened. "You think someone faked this? Briana, this isn't a race for the White House. It's a city mayor's job. Thomson's bank job probably pays more. The only reason he wanted to be mayor was for the prestige and power. I was a reluctant candidate from the start. No. I don't believe anyone faked the photo. Why are you so interested in Cecil Thomson's dirty laundry, anyway?"

She put the photo back on the table so she could avoid looking at Patrick. "I was trying to find a way to end the antipathy between the two of you."

"Well, your chances aren't great." He sighed and leaned back. "We talk about this stuff all day at work. Can we have a Saturday night off?"

"Yes. Of course. Sorry. Can I just say one more thing?

On Monday, I'm going to put in for a transfer. If you want to put in a good word for me with Max Zirinsky, I know there are a few positions in the police department that I'd enjoy."

Patrick grinned at her, relief and plain joy shining from his eyes. "I've got some positions you might enjoy, too." He laughed when she rolled her eyes. "Come here."

She was delighted to comply.

She rose slowly, irresistibly pulled toward him. How had they managed to hold off all the days and nights since the elevator escapade?

Since she didn't think the arm of her upholstered wicker armchair would hold her weight—at least that's the excuse she gave herself—she eased onto Patrick's lap and kissed him.

It was an easy kiss, meant to be the prelude to something very different from what they'd experienced in the elevator. For one thing, they had her apartment to spread out in, and for another, they weren't feeling their lives were in danger. But perhaps best of all, they had all night.

As though he'd read her mind, Patrick said, "You know what's been driving me crazy?"

Wanting her, she hoped. "What?"

"I don't know what you look like." His voice was already husky. "I know what you feel like, I know the scent of you, the taste of you." He nibbled her ear to illustrate his point. "But I have no idea what you look like naked."

She bent awkwardly as she tried to kiss him. They were going to either end up on her living room floor or make a move for the bed before it was too late.

Maybe later she'd go for the living room floor. This time, she wanted all the comforts.

So she took his hand and hauled him to his feet, then led him to her room.

Once more she congratulated herself on her housecleaning binge this morning. The sheets on the bed were fresh, the bathroom sparkled and all her junk was put away. She didn't live like a slob by any means, but today her place was as neat as it ever got. Not that Patrick seemed bothered about her decor. She suspected that if she put her hands over his eyes and asked him to describe anything about her apartment, he'd be stumped.

And for all the right reasons. Since he'd entered her home, he'd had eyes only for her.

His gaze was so intense that she shivered as he stepped close to her and reached for her shirt.

They undressed each other slowly. Watching him watch her strip off her blouse was as erotic as the most exquisite foreplay. He traced the lacy cups of her bra with a fingertip, leaving a trail of goose bumps in its wake, then slid the shirt slowly off her shoulders so it slipped to the floor like a dropped handkerchief.

He seemed undecided whether to go for bra or skirt next. She thought about reaching down for his belt buckle while he was busy making up his mind, but she felt curiously lazy, and decided she'd wait her turn.

The same index finger traced the line where her breasts met, tracked down over the bra and then followed the center line of her ribs in an invisible path that crossed her belly button and ended at the waistband of her short denim skirt.

He unzipped the skirt and she wriggled it past her hips.

He kissed her again, rubbing against her, and she decided he had far too many clothes on, when she was wearing so few. With a tug and a yank, she had his T-shirt out of his shorts and halfway up his belly. He stepped back a little and raised his arms so she could finish the job.

Mmm. Oh, yes. Mmm-hmm. She loved a hairy chest, and he had a terrific one. Lots of dark curls from his collarbone spreading over his nicely developed pecs and tapering down to his ribs.

A gold medallion of some sort nestled against his sternum. "What's this?" she asked, touching the medal.

"St. Christopher."

"It's nice." And it was. Intricately detailed, and warm from his body.

While she admired the medallion, he unsnapped her bra and pulled it away before she realized he was going to.

"Apricot," he mumbled with satisfaction.

"I beg your pardon?"

"Apricot. I had a bet with myself what color your nipples would be. They're a little more on the brown side than I'd guessed, but I had the right general palette."

"I can't believe you've been thinking about the color of my nipples."

He grinned at her. "They match the color of your cheeks when you blush."

As she was doing now.

He flipped back the bedcover and laid her on her back, then he slid his thumbs into the waistband of her panties and eased them down.

A single shiver passed over her from crown to toe as the silky material slid down her legs. The sheets were cool and crisp to the touch, smelling faintly of lavender linen spray.

He kissed her slowly and thoroughly, beginning with her

mouth and heading slowly south as though she were a long-denied treat and his diet was over.

"I think you even taste like apricots," he said, as he toyed with her breasts before sucking one sensitive tip right into his mouth.

Oh, what that man could do with his lips and tongue. He kissed her skin everywhere, bringing it to tingling life. Slow and meticulous, he seemed intent on kissing every inch of her.

"Oh, Patrick," she sighed.

"I didn't take enough time with you in the elevator," he murmured against her ribs. "I was in too much of a hurry, too eager."

"I loved what happened in the elevator."

He grinned up at her. "Me, too. But this time, we've got all night."

And he was as good as his word. He kissed her everywhere, and what he wasn't kissing, he was touching, stroking, learning with his hands.

She was close to begging him to take her, when he slipped her thighs apart and put his mouth just there. She felt zapped—shocked to the core—and tiny helpless cries escaped her.

He licked her until she couldn't hold back, and every part of her exploded; fireworks burst behind her eyelids and she let out a sob of relief.

Only then did he sheath himself. As he positioned himself at the still-pulsing entrance to her body, he smiled down at her with great tenderness and held her gaze as he entered her slowly.

Even though they'd been intimate in the elevator, this

was completely different. It was light, and they'd made this decision as consenting adults, not as adrenaline-pumped earthquake victims. He felt so right moving inside her, reaching all her lonely places, that she longed to close her eyes and savor every sensation. But somehow she knew how important it was for him to look into her eyes, so she kept them open for him, ignoring the quiver of fear that such intimacy caused.

When he started moving faster, she lost her grip on conscious thought and concentrated instead of hanging on to him. He was beautiful, decent and gorgeous. If only she could stop her feelings from going too deep.

If only it weren't too late.

His eyes darkened, his breathing harshened, his movements became half-crazed. As climax rocked her, she set off his explosion and they seemed to melt together in one perfect moment.

"I love you," he said as he poured himself into her body.

CHAPTER TWELVE

I LOVE YOU. The words echoed in the air along with their labored breathing and pounding hearts.

Briana wished Patrick hadn't said those dangerous words, those dangerous, magic words, as she played her fingers through her lover's hair, feeling warmth coming off him in waves.

It was a moment of such perfect contentment, she wished she could make it last. He loved her.

After a minute or two, he raised himself up on his forearms so he could look down into her face. Cupping her cheek in his palm, he kissed her softly on the lips. "I didn't mean to blurt out my feelings so soon," he said. "They're true, though. I do love you."

"Well, I'm glad it's not an automatic reflex thing, every time you climax."

He chuckled. "No. Usually I'm not so articulate. If I'd thought about it, I wouldn't have said it, I guess, but I didn't think."

"Oh, Patrick. I love you, too."

What a tangled web she'd woven, and hadn't she become well ensnared in it? The man she was meant to entrap had trapped her, body and heart.

"You do?" He seemed almost as surprised as relieved.

She smiled up at him. "I love you. I love Dylan and Fiona, I even love poor disaster-plagued Courage Bay."

"That's good, but I haven't even had a chance to date you properly yet. You may think you love me, but wait until you see my woman-getting arsenal. You'll be under attack and won't know what hit you."

"Under attack, huh?" she said, feeling girlishly silly and delighted at the idea.

"That's right. Morning." He kissed her lips. "Noon." He kissed the spot where her breasts met. "And night." As though he couldn't resist, he came back to her mouth and kissed her again, deeply.

"What form will this attack take?" she wondered aloud, loving this fun-loving, sweet, sweet man, so different from the suit-and-tie mayor.

"My arsenal is mostly secret. However, I think it's fair to say there will be wining and dining."

She considered. "Two fine weapons."

"I don't think flowers would be going too far."

"A woman always likes to receive a bouquet now and then," she agreed.

"That's more the mental siege, to break down your resistance, before I step up the attack and move into the physical phase."

"Oh, you're planning to bully me?"

He shook his head. "Woo you."

"I like the sound of wooing."

"After the wining, dining and flowers, there will be some very physical wooing, don't you worry."

"You're sounding awfully confident."

He kissed her again, a nice loud smacker. "Actually, I'm not, but my heart's gone now, and since I can't get it back, I'll just have to get you along with it."

"Oh," she said, feeling a prickle at her eyelids that surprised the heck out of her, "that is so sweet."

"I know I'm pushing you, and rushing you and pressuring you and doing everything I shouldn't, but I need you to realize that I'm also a package deal. You can't have me in your life and not have Fiona and Dylan."

She snuggled up to him and kissed his chin, then the tip of his nose, and then his lips, which still tasted a little of her. "In case you hadn't noticed, I'm already in your life. And theirs."

Even though she'd tried to resist him, Dylan was as up front about his own brand of wooing as his dad, and Fiona didn't have to do a thing to steal her heart. She'd fallen for the little tyke the first minute she saw her.

Her happiness was slightly tarnished by a flickering thought for her uncle, but she pushed it aside.

She couldn't have fallen in love with a man who wasn't trustworthy, and she couldn't go on loving him without admitting how she'd come to work for him.

Phew, it wasn't going to be easy, admitting that she'd taken the job under false pretenses. But when she explained why, and shared the results of her investigation, she hoped he'd understand that although she'd joined his staff with an ulterior motive, she would never have done anything to hurt him or his family.

Suddenly, a sense of urgency gripped her. As soon as she saw Joe Carlton, she'd tell Patrick everything.

They made love again, their newly expressed feelings

adding a poignancy and intensity she'd never experienced before. "I never thought I could be this happy again," he said when he was buried deep inside her body and they were as close as two people can be.

By the time they'd finished round two, which had somehow morphed into round three without a break, Briana was feeling emotionally and physically sated.

"Are you hungry?" she asked.

He narrowed his eyes at her. "That depends. If we have to leave this apartment to find food, then no, I'm not hungry. I'm too tired to move. I may never move again."

"How about if I told you I already have a salad and chicken breast prepared?" She wasn't the only one who needed refueling. They'd both been pretty acrobatic that last round.

"In that case, I'm famished."

She chuckled. "I also have a freezer full of stuff. I have domestic urges," she admitted, as though it were a shameful secret. "When I'm upset or thinking deeply about things, I always cook. And since I live alone, well, like I said, I have a freezer full of stuff."

He dragged himself out of bed and stepped into his shorts, leaving his chest bare. Which was just the way she liked it. If she had her way, he'd always go bare-chested. In fact, she might make it a rule for his entry into her apartment, she thought with a foolish sense of burgeoning happiness. Or maybe it was a burgeoning sense of foolish happiness. Could she be this lucky?

Tomorrow, she was going back to Acadia Springs, and whatever she learned there, she decided she was going to tell Patrick everything.

"You know what I can't believe?" Patrick said over the salad and chicken breast and the homemade bread she'd taken out of the freezer and warmed.

"What?"

"Shannon really likes you."

Briana almost choked on a cherry tomato. "If that's like, I never, ever want to be on her bad side."

He chuckled. "She's mellowed, believe me. You should have seen her before she and John got together."

"Patrick, the woman threatened me with violence if I ever hurt you or your kids."

"Remind me to buy her a bigger Christmas present," he said with a grin.

She tried to kick him under the table, but her aim wasn't great.

"You know," he said, catching her hand in his, "people hurt each other. It happens. You can't not risk your heart on the chance it could get broken."

She nodded, although he had no idea she'd been sent here to deliberately hurt him.

"Janie hurt me. And the kids. She never meant to, of course. No one plans to die suddenly one morning out of the blue. When she was first gone, I used to wish I'd never met her. Then I wouldn't have had to face her dying." His voice grew a tad husky, and he paused to take a sip of wine. "But I wouldn't have Dylan and Fiona if I hadn't loved Janie, and I can't imagine the world without them."

She felt tears prick her eyelids. "And she was able to leave a part of herself behind." How could she be so lucky that such a man had fallen in love with her? "It must have been so difficult for you to lose her when the poor kids were so young." She recalled Shannon's earlier words about Janie's pregnancy.

"It was hell. Pure, unadulterated hell. I was angry at her for a long time. You know, those stages of grief everyone tells you about and you don't believe you're in?"

She didn't completely, of course, but she nodded anyway, wanting him to continue.

"After I finally got it through my head that she was gone, I was furious that she'd left me. Furious that she'd left the kids." He shook his head, broke apart a piece of bread but didn't eat it. "It sounds awful to even say that, but it's true. I was mad at her, mad at God, mad at the world."

He looked up at Briana and smiled, the sad, wise smile of a man who's been through a tragedy and lived to talk about it. "I knew I was finally starting to heal when I realized how grateful I was to her for those kids."

She nodded and reached across the table to clasp his hand, so warm and leathery from all those years of firefighting. He squeezed back, linking their fingers. "Anyhow, I survived and the kids survived. Loving you is the same. There's risk involved. You could get sick. I could get sick. One of us could die. You could end up not being willing to take on another woman's children. I understand the risks and, for the first time in three years, I'm ready to take them."

The tears now filled her eyes. "I think I'm the luckiest woman in the world," she said. "I'm going to try so hard to make you happy."

"That's what I'm trying to tell you. Shannon had it wrong. So wrong. Hurt happens. Bad things happen. My happiness is not your responsibility. I love you. That's my choice."

"Right. I understand that. And I'm making a choice, too." She suddenly felt the need to lighten the atmosphere. "I'm making a choice to drag you back to bed."

They made love twice more during the night, and when she awoke in the morning, she found herself alone in bed. The noise of the shower had woken her. She pondered the idea of slipping out of bed and joining Patrick under the pounding spray, but felt too lazy.

Instead, she lay there, sleepily remembering last night. She knew she'd never forget it as long as she lived.

She dozed a little until he came out, fresh, damp and smelling of her shampoo. "I used one of your pink plastic razors," he said, rubbing his hand along his jaw as though it hurt. "Those things should be banned."

"They're not meant for men with sexy Irish beards," she informed him.

He stared down at her for a long moment, as though imprinting her face on his memory. This was how he'd look, she thought, if he was heading off to war and might never see her again. Torn between wanting to stay and knowing he had to leave.

"I have to go," he said, as though that were news.

"Do you want some coffee before you go? I could thaw some homemade muffins."

"I'd love to, but if I stay any longer, we'll end up back in that bed, and I'll be late getting the kids. I don't want them overstaying their welcome at Aunt Shannon's." He kissed her and grinned down at her. "We want her to volunteer again."

She nodded enthusiastically. "Soon, and often."

"See you tomorrow at the office."

"Right." Reality started to creep back, but Briana wouldn't let it. The day was sunny, she felt well-loved, and there was a nice drive ahead of her. By tonight, with luck, she'd know the name of the culprit who'd ruined her uncle's career, and it wouldn't be O'Shea.

Patrick kissed her quickly on the lips, but she wrapped her arms around his neck and pulled him down for a longer, sweeter goodbye kiss.

"I love you," he whispered, then drew away and left the room swiftly.

"I love you, too," she said.

CHAPTER THIRTEEN

THE SECOND DRIVE up to Acadia Springs was even more gorgeous than the first. She sang along to her favorite CDs, enjoyed the scenery and delighted in being newly in love. Since the retirement community was an hour inland, it was dryer and warmer than the coastal city she'd left.

As Briana drove, she mostly replayed scenes from the night before, warming with a glow of pleasure as she relived what had to be the most remarkable night of her life.

For the second time she pulled up in front of a neatly kept bungalow adjacent to a luscious green golf course. This time, she was pleased to see the drapes open, no papers on the front porch and a late-model Ford sitting in the garage. Having already worried about how she'd approach Joseph Carlton, she'd finally settled on the truth, or some version of it, anyway.

It seemed to her that lies had caused the trouble her uncle was in, and maybe the truth would be a good start for fixing things.

Consequently, when she rang the doorbell of number 233 Palm Avenue at two o'clock that Sunday afternoon, she was ready to come out about who she really was.

A woman in her seventies answered the door, wearing

a bright sun-orange baseball cap and tennis gear. "Oh," she said, looking startled. "I thought you were my doubles partner."

"No, ma'am," Briana answered with a smile. "My name is Briana Bliss. I work for the city of Courage Bay. I'm looking for retired officer Joseph Carlton of the Courage Bay police department. Would he be in?"

"Yes, of course. Come right in."

"Thank you." As she stepped inside, the nervousness she'd tried to keep at bay on the drive up returned. She had a feeling that, finally, she was going to get the truth.

The woman disappeared down a hall, and a few minutes later Briana heard an older man say, "It's all right, May. You go on and play tennis."

A short muffled conversation took place, out of her sight, and then an older man came down the hall toward her. Briana would have guessed ex-military from his stern bearing and upright posture if she hadn't known he was a former police officer.

His hair was salt-and-pepper and a thin mustache graced his upper lip. Behind his glasses, his gray eyes were wary.

He looked at her a long moment, then, with a small sigh and an infinitesimal slump of his shoulders, he motioned her toward the living room.

"You *are* the Officer Carlton who served on the Courage Bay police force in the eighties?" Briana asked.

The older man nodded, gesturing her to a floral couch in greens and yellows. The decor was department-store Colonial, and everything was sparkling clean.

"Yes, I served in the eighties. And the seventies. And most of the sixties, too. I retired in nineteen ninety-two."

Before he sank into what was obviously his favorite chair, a green wing chair with a footstool in front and a carefully folded newspaper on the polished side table, he paused. "Would you like some iced tea?"

"That would be wonderful, thank you. I'm a little thirsty after the drive up here."

"I'll get it," came his wife's voice.

"Then you go play tennis," her husband called. "This young lady and I will be fine."

"I…I don't know what to call you. Retired Officer Carlton doesn't sound quite right."

"Call me Joe."

She smiled. "And I'm Briana. Briana Bliss."

"Bliss." He shook his head. "Not a surname I recognize."

"I just recently moved to Courage Bay, Joe. I work for the mayor. The new mayor. Patrick O'Shea. I'm his administrative assistant."

A rusty chuckle shook her companion. "Now, O'Shea's a name I know well. Good kids, but they played their fair share of pranks. I'd heard young Patrick was the mayor down there, after the old one made a fool of himself."

"Well, it's sort of the election that I wanted to talk to you about."

"Never mingled in politics myself."

"Right. It's not directly about politics. What I wanted to ask you about involves an arrest you made in the eighties. I don't know if you'll even remember any of the details, but I thought I'd ask anyway." She'd also brought a copy of the article, including the grainy arrest photo from the *Courage Bay Sentinel*.

May Carlton came into the room with two chilled

glasses of iced tea in crystal tumblers. Thin slices of lemon floated on top.

"Thank you," Briana said gratefully, and sipped the cool drink. May set a coaster on the table in front of her. "There's more iced tea in the fridge if you want it, dear." Then, after kissing her husband on the forehead, she left.

"You go on, now," Joe said to her.

There was a short silence. "I understand you celebrated your fiftieth wedding anniversary," she said. "Congratulations."

"Thanks. How did you know?"

She explained about coming up the week before, when he and his wife were away, and he nodded. "You must have something pressing on your mind to make this trip twice in the space of a week."

"It's not urgent, but I believe it's important." She took the neatly folded photocopy out of her bag and passed it over. Joe Carlton studied the photo carefully for several long seconds and nodded. Then he raised his eyes to her.

He still had cop eyes, she realized. They missed nothing.

"This is Cecil Thomson. I arrested him in 1984. A misdemeanor."

She felt as though someone had kicked her. For a long time there was only silence punctuated by muted traffic sounds from the main road and the ticking of a clock.

"How can you remember it so clearly?" She was startled and it must have showed. "That was more than twenty years ago. You must have performed hundreds, thousands of arrests in your time. How can you be so certain you remember this one?"

"Because Cecil Thomson was a prominent man, even

then. He wasn't president of the bank back in those days, but he was already a councilman."

"Right." Her stomach was starting to feel funny, as though she might be coming down with something. "What happened?"

"What's your interest in this?"

How much to tell? How much to withhold? "Some damaging information about Councilman Thomson was leaked to the press during the mayoralty race. There's been some suggestion..." She looked over at the older man whose eyes had seen so much and decided to trust him. "I'd like to keep this visit, and this conversation, confidential for the moment. There's been a...suggestion made that the arrest and the photograph were false. That they were planted to ruin Councilman Thomson's bid to become Courage Bay's mayor."

Joe chuckled, then he laughed out loud. But it wasn't the kind of laugh that made you want to join in. It had a bitter sound. The feeling in her stomach grew worse.

"Oh, it was real all right. The photo. The arrest. The whole ball of wax."

"But—but I don't understand. Why was he never charged? And why did it take twenty years to come to light?"

"You look like a nice young woman, but if you're involved in any kind of politics, even as the mayor's secretary, you must know there's dirty tricks even at the lowest level."

"I hate to think that's true, but I suppose you're right," she said.

The old man nodded, then settled back to tell his story.

"I was out on the beat one summer evening in eighty-four. It was a quiet night. A couple of kids had a few open beers on the beach. I could smell marijuana, but they'd got rid of that before I caught them, so all I could do was give them the usual talking to about drinking underage and then I drove them home to their parents."

He stopped to sip his tea. Briana was amazed at how clear his recall was of an incident two decades old.

"On my way back to the precinct, I cruised The Lair, which was and still is the meanest part of Victory Park."

Briana nodded.

"Prostitutes hung out there. Some drug deals went down. There were bar brawls and plenty of petty theft. I was doing a routine drive through and I saw a couple in a car. I might not have noticed them, but the car didn't belong in the area. It was a new model Cadillac."

Her heart sank still further. Her uncle had always driven Cadillacs. Always. He got a new model every four years without fail, and Aunt Irene got the four-year-old one.

Joe cleared his throat and looked uncomfortable. "Well, I could see inside the car that there was a couple going at it, so I got out the camera and turned on the flash. There was a lewd act happening in a public place, and the woman was a prostitute I knew well enough. I'd arrested her before."

"And the man?" Her throat felt so dry and scratchy she could barely get the words out. She knew, of course. Realized that on some level she'd suspected this for a while but had refused to believe it.

"It was Cecil Thomson. I knew him pretty well, too. So I snapped their photo, and Cecil, well, he got himself pretty riled up. When I look back on it now, I think I probably would have let him off with a warning—it was a first offense and I'd never seen him down in that part of town before—but he got belligerent on me. I remember I smelled booze, so I guess he'd had a few drinks and wasn't acting too smart. Anyhow, I arrested the pair of them and took them down to the station, filled out the paperwork and attached the photograph to the file. Cecil Thomson must have sobered up some by then, because he demanded the phone, and guess who he called?"

"His lawyer?"

Joe shook his head and his mouth twisted in a cynical grimace. "No, he did not call his lawyer. He called the police chief. They were great buddies in those days. Old Chief Conway's gone now. Died of lung cancer. Let me just say, I don't mourn his passing."

"So, Un— So, Cecil Thomson called Chief Conway. What did the police chief do?"

Joe gave another humorless laugh. "He let Cecil Thomson go. Told me I'd been too quick to judge, that there was insufficient evidence and we wouldn't be taking this one to trial. He even let the hooker go free."

"But..." Briana's head was reeling. "He was the police chief. Surely it was his duty to support his officers."

"That's not the way he saw it."

"But how could he stop you going above his head, or even to the newspapers if you'd wanted to?"

"I guess he knew I wouldn't do either of those things."

"You mean you've kept this secret all these years?"

Joe Carlton stared down at his hands, and suddenly she wished she didn't have to press him for answers. He obviously didn't want to talk about this, something which he confirmed when he said, "Here's the part of the story I wish I didn't have to tell you, but it wouldn't be right not to. I got a promotion the next week. Now, I was in line for one and sure as hell deserved it, but I always thought the timing was too much of a coincidence. Yeah. I kept my mouth shut, and I probably would have anyway. But I also took the promotion." He shook his head. "Never felt right about it. But I had a wife and kids to support. And that's the story."

Her head was whirling. But one huge piece of the puzzle was still missing. "It's not quite the end of the story, though. Why did you leak it to the papers twenty years later? Was it for revenge?"

He chortled. "That's a good one. If I'd ever thought of it, I probably wouldn't have had the guts to leak information the way they love to do these days. No. The photo from the arrest disappeared very conveniently that same night. I guess the chief figured that if I did try anything, it would be my word against his and the good councilman. But I'd taken a couple of pictures, see? I always did. In case one didn't turn out."

He sat back and sipped more tea. "I clipped the clearest one to the file and I kept the backup."

"Why?"

"I suppose that photograph was a reminder to myself that I wasn't any better than the next man."

"So you kept that photo all these years?"

"Sure did. I probably should have tossed it when I retired, but I'd mostly forgotten about it by then. My daughter was up here a few months back. She's married to a fellow that works for the *Sentinel.* She was going through some old boxes in the storage locker, looking for I don't know what, and she found that picture. Like I said, I'd almost forgotten about it. Well, after she got through wondering what I was doing with a picture of two people going at it, I told her the story. I guess maybe it eased my conscience a little.

"I never expected she'd take that picture with her and run straight to her husband." Joe stopped to rub his jaw and a sly twinkle flickered in his eyes. "At least, I don't think I did." He chuckled a little. "Maybe I wasn't sorry, though, that the truth finally came out."

Oh, and was the truth ever coming out. She felt ill. Faint and nauseous. Her uncle had always been someone she admired and looked up to. He loved his wife, and he loved her. How could he go to a prostitute in the first place? Then use political influence to get the charge dropped, and then lie to his own wife and niece about the incident? The only truthful thing he'd told them was that he believed Patrick had planted the story.

And he'd jumped to that conclusion because he knew all about political dirty tricks and influence peddling.

And the irony was, that was the only part of the story that wasn't true.

Her uncle had been wrong on so many levels. Patrick hadn't set Uncle Cecil up. Patrick hadn't known a thing about the arrest until he'd read it in the paper. It was the arresting officer's son-in-law who'd made a timely news story out of an averted scandal.

The only person who'd been set up, she now saw, was her own gullible self.

"Are you all right over there?"

She'd dropped her head in her hand and closed her eyes as the shock of the truth hit her. "Yes. Yes, thank you. I'm fine. I—I'm glad to hear that Mayor Patrick O'Shea had nothing to do with starting false rumors." That at least was true.

"If that mayor of yours is anything like he was ten years ago, when he was a young fireman, why, he's as honest as the day is long. He comes from a good family, but he was one of the biggest sticklers for honesty and integrity I ever saw." The older man leaned forward. "After the scandal with the last mayor, I'm awfully glad you've got a good man doing the job now. Especially since you've had all that trouble down there."

"Yes," Briana said, smiling shakily. "Yes, Mayor O'Shea is a good man." And she wished the same could be said of her uncle.

Silence stretched between them. "I'm not sure I can tell you any more."

"You've been very helpful," she said, rising to her feet. "Thank you."

"I'm not going to tell you it was a pleasure, but it was a duty, and I'm glad I've discharged that duty."

She looked at him and saw a fine man who'd done something he wasn't altogether proud of, something he'd been forced to do because of her uncle. She felt like crying. "Is there…I hate to ask you this, but do you think I could talk to your daughter?"

"You think I made all this up?" Joe had risen, too, and now he was staring at her as if she were nuts.

"No. Of course I don't think you made it up, but I have to be sure. A lot is at stake here."

He glanced at her with those cop's eyes again. "Knowing my daughter, she'd be more than happy to talk about anything." He reached for the pencil that perched on top of his newspaper. He'd been doing the crossword puzzle, she saw, and had more than half of the squares filled in. She was sorry she'd had to interrupt such a quiet Sunday afternoon activity with reminders of an incident in the past that he'd rather forget. He tore off a corner of the paper and carefully wrote down a name and phone number. "That's their home. Joan will talk to you. Tell her I said it's okay."

"Thank you, Joe. Thank you very much."

"Well, I'm ashamed I had any part in that, but I'm glad the truth is finally coming out."

"It can't have been easy for you," she said, sorry he was still beating himself up over something that had happened two decades earlier. "You had a family. I'm sure you needed the job."

Joe shook his head at her. "Young lady, if there's one thing I've learned in my life, it's that doing the right thing is always the right thing to do. I've regretted keeping quiet for a lot of years." He smiled at her. "One of the nice things about getting old is you're allowed to give a lot of unwanted advice. But here's a piece of advice I hope you'll take to heart. Don't ever make the mistake of compromising your integrity for someone else."

She felt tears spring to her eyes at his words.

Too late. She'd already compromised her integrity by agreeing to go undercover in Patrick's office with the express purpose of destroying his career.

Loyalty and integrity. She'd misplaced the first and compromised the second.

She only hoped she wasn't too late to act with both.

After saying her goodbyes to Joe, she realized she was going to have to confront her uncle before she did anything else.

Her thoughts were grim on the drive back to Courage Bay. She'd imagined a lot of scenarios, but never had it seemed possible that the uncle who'd helped her so much when she was growing up would use her so despicably.

She was furious on her own behalf, and she was equally furious on her aunt's. How could he profess to love that woman so deeply and do something so awful behind her back? She could still barely believe he *had* gone with a hooker. Had it been a regular thing? she wondered. Her poor aunt.

Yes, she needed to see Patrick and come clean about what she'd done, but she had to see Uncle Cecil first.

Then she was going to have to tell Patrick the truth about why she'd applied to be his admin assistant.

She really hoped his love was blind. She needed him to be blind to her faults when she finally told him the truth.

CHAPTER FOURTEEN

PATRICK HADN'T FELT this good in years. Three years to be precise, he realized as he drove away from Briana's place and a night he'd never forget.

After living through grief, and then getting on with life because he had to, because he had kids to raise and a job to perform, he felt amazed to be experiencing this incredible emotion he'd almost forgotten.

Happiness.

Oh, he'd been content for the past couple of years, with healthy children, a wonderful family and a challenging career. But he'd felt sort of numb. And here, when he'd least suspected it, he'd gone and fallen head over heels in love.

He felt corny even thinking about it, never mind the fact that he was whistling along to a love song on his car radio by the Bee Gees. But after almost forgetting he was capable of it, he'd rediscovered love. Briana had brought him that goofy-smile-on-your-face kind of happiness that comes with new love.

Maybe he shouldn't have sprung his feelings on her like that. He hadn't intended the words to spill out, but he'd been feeling so damned good that the words came out before he could stop them.

At the time, he'd felt more than a little foolish, especially when she hadn't blurted those magic words right back, but now he was glad he'd admitted his love. He liked everything out in the open. He loved Briana and his feelings were honest. He was proud to love her, so why shouldn't he tell her?

He planned to tell her often, he decided with a grin that seriously impaired his whistling, so she'd better get used to it.

He picked up his kids, and the single-eyebrow-raised look from his kid sister told him his newly admitted feelings were blazoned all over his face. Not that he minded Shannon knowing how he felt, but he'd be a lot happier to go public once Briana worked for someone else.

"Dad!" Fiona squealed when he entered the kitchen, where they were just finishing up breakfast. "I missed you." She ran up and threw her arms around him. He lifted her up, anyway—sticky fingers, syrup-streaked cheeks and all—for a good-morning hug.

"I missed you, too, Fiona."

Dylan, more manly and restrained, said, "Hi, Dad," and continued to eat. Patrick ruffled his hair and took the mug of coffee John had already filled and held out to him. He nodded his thanks.

Fiona ran back to the table to finish her breakfast and Patrick sipped his coffee.

The three adults took their coffee out on to the back deck.

"I'm guessing my little ploy to give you two some couple time worked," Shannon said with no pretense at discretion.

"Really?" He tried to keep a straight face, but it was impossible when she looked so desperate to hear all about his night with Briana.

"Yeah. And I'm guessing someone I know owes me a big fat favor!"

"Really?"

Shannon narrowed her eyes at him. "If you keep saying 'Really?' you're going to be wearing that coffee, big bro."

He pulled her to him in a half headlock, half hug. "Okay. I owe you big time."

"Back off, Shannon," John said. "If Patrick wants to tell you, he will."

Shannon merely shot him a mischievous look and went right back to grilling her brother.

"When she ran out of there like the place was on fire, I thought it was a no go."

"Well, it would have been, but your suave and persuasive older brother—that would be me—drove over to her place and convinced her that a date with me was a good thing."

"Date? Is that what they call it?"

He squeezed a little tighter. "That's what we're calling it."

She pulled away, laughing. "Okay, okay. From the look on your face, the 'date' was spectacular."

He allowed a little of the smugness he felt this morning to wash over him. "Oh, yeah. It was spectacular all right."

She nodded. "Are you worried about people talking? I mean, because she works in your office?"

"First off, no one knows except you. So if any of this leaks out, I'll know who to kill. Got that?"

She threw up her hands. "Hey, I'm the good guy, remember? I took your kids for a sleepover so you could enjoy a night of *luv.*" She held her clasped hands at her chest and gazed up at the ceiling.

He ignored her immature antics and answered her question. "Briana's going to put in for a transfer to a different job. Until that's done, obviously, she and I have to keep things under wraps. I'm not happy about this, of course. Of all women to fall for..." He shook his head.

"Hey, you can't help who you fall for." She rolled her eyes. "Look at me!"

Patrick laughed out loud. "You and John couldn't be better suited or more *in luv,* so give it up, kid."

"So," Shannon said, "you're going to play it cool until she gets this transfer?"

"That's right."

Shannon snorted. "You give it up, kid. You're crazy in love with the woman. You're never going to be able to stay away from her."

Patrick was secretly worried that his sister was right. Even though he'd only been apart from Briana for less than an hour, he missed her. He wanted to call her, just to hear her voice, to see what she was doing. He'd forgotten to ask what she was up to today.

Once the kids had washed up and collected their night gear, he packed them straight off to Dylan's Little League practice, and once that was over, treated them to lunch at a family restaurant. He chose the location because it was pretty close to Briana's place. He figured this was still the weekend, so she wasn't officially his employee again until tomorrow.

Knowing he was stretching his own ethics, he called her on his cell phone anyway, deciding a spur-of-the-minute invitation to lunch when they were right in her neighborhood was perfectly appropriate. They'd be well-chaperoned by his children. But Briana wasn't there.

He felt a little disappointed, but figured she'd gone out to exercise or shop or something.

Later in the afternoon, he called again to see if she wanted to come over for a family supper, and once more got her voice mail. He hadn't left a message the first time, not wanting to appear too eager, but this time he did.

"Hi," he said to the machine. "It's Patrick. The kids and I wanted to invite you for dinner, but I guess you're not there. Call me back when you get in. Bye."

It was strange that she'd been out all day, but he didn't own the woman. They'd spent the night together—that didn't give him the right to know her every movement. Still, he'd feel better when she called back.

BRIANA WAS FURIOUS. Her uncle had used her and betrayed her, but underneath her anger, she was heartbroken. She'd believed in Cecil Thomson. He'd been almost like a father to her. She'd trusted him. Loved him and her aunt. And he'd used her.

Manipulated her.

Lied to her.

And all so that she would manipulate and lie to the decent wonderful man she'd fallen in love with.

As the miles between Acadia Springs and Courage Bay disappeared, she grew angrier. And what about her poor Aunt Irene? How would she react when she found out the vile truth?

The first thing she did when she arrived home was to call Joe Carlton's daughter. Before she confronted her uncle, Briana wanted to be absolutely certain that Joe Carlton's story was true. Right away she explained who she was, and Joan said, "Yes, I know. Dad told me you'd be calling."

"I'm really sorry to bother you on a Sunday night, but could I see that photograph?"

"I don't see why not. You can't take it with you, though. I don't trust that Cecil Thomson not to try and destroy it if he finds out where it is."

"No. I won't take it anywhere."

There was a message on her voice mail from Patrick, but right now Briana didn't feel able to talk to him without sobbing her heart out and telling him the whole story.

Except she didn't yet have the whole story. Not the final chapter anyway. Or, she supposed, it was really the first chapter she needed in this sordid tale.

She found Joan's house without difficulty and was invited in to a cozy kitchen where the smell of lasagna permeated the air.

Joan had a file folder sitting on the kitchen table already. Briana's hands shook slightly as she opened it. Inside was a copy of the arrest report, mug shots of her uncle, looking younger and more disheveled than she'd ever seen him, and his companion.

The hooker was a blowsy woman with long bleached hair and too much lipstick, as though she'd reapplied it for her mug shot.

But the third photo was the one she'd really come to see. It was still a little blurry, but there was no doubt that the startled-looking man was her uncle, and the woman peering up from his lap was the blond hooker.

"You're sure this is all…accurate?" she asked Joan's husband, Tom.

"Believe me, we're very careful about libel at the *Sentinel*, especially when a public figure's involved. My paper wouldn't have run that story if we weren't certain it was true. And while there were a few letters to the editor from Councilman Thomson, lambasting the paper for its scurrilous reporting, he never sued for libel. Never even threatened it, because he knows the story is true."

"But we keep this file well hidden, just in case," Joan added.

Briana felt the last of her hope that her uncle might still prove to be innocent fall away.

"You seem awfully interested in this story about the councilor," Tom said, gazing at her with the sharp speculation of a reporter whose newshound nose is twitching. "Any particular reason why Mayor Patrick O'Shea's assistant is researching Cecil Thomson? The same Cecil Thomson who's blocked the mayor's efforts for more funding?"

Darn it. She'd been so all-fired determined to get to the truth that she'd forgotten to be discreet. Thinking up a good reason for her interest was not an easy task.

She shook her head. "This has nothing to do with the funding crisis. I'm working on a…" *What?* "Well, an ad hoc ethics committee. I wanted to research recent scandals involving local politicians."

"Interesting timing, looking for dirt on Councilman Thomson right when he and your boss are pitted against each other."

"The two things are *not* related," she insisted. "Please, I need you to keep this meeting off the record."

"Any reason why I should?"

What could she offer him in return for his silence? Nothing he'd care about.

Her gaze fell on Joan, who was watching with interest. "I can't explain right now, but what I'm doing will probably mean the end of Cecil Thomson's career," she said, her voice shaking a little at the knowledge that this was true. "It's personal."

Joan stared at her for a moment and nodded. "Tom won't print anything."

"Now, wait just a minute!" her husband said.

"Remember," Joan said, turning to him and jabbing him in the chest, "I gave you that picture and the story on a silver platter. If I tell you not to blab about a social visit Ms. Bliss paid to *me,* not you, then you don't blab."

The reporter didn't look happy with his wife's logic.

Hoping to prevent him going off half-cocked, Briana said, "How about this? If Councilman Thomson quits because of my investigation, you'll be the first to know."

"A scoop, huh?" he said with a wily grin.

"Yes. A scoop."

"Okay. Deal." He stepped forward and shook Briana's hand. "I expect you to keep your word."

She smiled sadly. "Don't worry. I work for a man who believes fiercely in truth and honesty. I won't let you down." She wished the same could be said of herself in reference to Patrick.

Her last stop of the evening was the one she least wanted to make.

After parking outside her aunt and uncle's house, Briana walked up the path and rang the doorbell.

From inside, she heard the muted sounds of a television program, which meant they were probably both home and not entertaining. Good.

Her aunt opened the door and smiled with delight. "Briana, what a nice surprise. Come in, dear. Have you eaten? I've got some fresh tuna and salad left from our dinner."

"Thanks. I'm not hungry. I'd like to talk to you and Uncle Cecil."

"Why, whatever's happened?" her aunt asked, looking at her searchingly. "Honey, do you feel all right? Did that awful Patrick O'Shea do something to upset you?"

Briana wanted to laugh hysterically and had to force herself to calm down. "Please, I really need to talk to Uncle Cecil."

"Well, sure, honey." Looking concerned, Aunt Irene walked her into the living room, snapping on a light and making sure the drapes were closed tight. Then she went to fetch Uncle Cecil.

He walked in a couple of minutes later. "Why, Briana, what's this—"

She glared at him, letting everything she now knew and thought about him show in her eyes. "How could you betray Aunt Irene and me? How could you?"

Uncle Cecil flinched, then glanced away, his ruddy complexion darkening. With a sigh, he lowered his bulk heavily into a chair.

"It's time you stopped lying," Briana told him. "To your wife, to me, to everybody."

"Lying? Why, Briana, whatever is the matter? Cecil?"

"I'm going to tell Patrick O'Shea everything," Briana said. "I came here tonight, first, out of courtesy and out of loyalty for all you've done for me in the past. But tomorrow I'm going to tell my boss how I took the job of his admin assistant in order to trap him into an indiscretion and ruin his career." The words almost choked her and she felt the first tear blur her vision. Resolutely she blinked it back. "He's an honest, decent man, Uncle Cecil. You should be ashamed of yourself."

"Oh, Cecil, what have you done?" her aunt asked.

He rubbed a hand over his face and looked suddenly older and smaller somehow. "Sit down, dear," he said gently to his wife. Then he turned back to Briana.

"How did you find out?" he said.

"I knew after I'd only worked for Patrick for a little while that he was incapable of the kind of deceit you accused him of. So, because I believed in you, because of my loyalty to you, I decided to investigate myself and find out who'd spread those awful lies about you."

Her voice was rising, she couldn't seem to help it, and the tears were only held at bay by the force of her will.

Her uncle didn't answer, so Briana continued. "I tracked down the source of that story in the newspaper. I interviewed the arresting officer, and he told me how, after you were arrested, you called your friend, Chief Conway, the police chief of the time. He made sure no charges were ever laid. He even managed to dispose of the photographic evidence of your misconduct." She was starting to sound like a legal textbook, but she didn't care. "You were good friends, you and the chief, back in the eighties, weren't you?"

Her uncle still said nothing, merely stared down at his hands, clasped between his knees.

"Even after I interviewed the arresting officer, I still wasn't a hundred percent convinced." She sniffed. "I saw the picture. With nothing blacked out."

He flinched at that.

"Chief Conway destroyed the photo that the arresting officer included in his report, but he didn't know there was a second photograph. Officer Carlton kept it for all these years."

"But—but those were lies, Cecil. It was all a lie!" Her aunt began to weep, and for a moment Briana felt guilty for the pain she was causing. But she wasn't the one causing pain, she reminded herself. Uncle Cecil had used her to try to cover up his own wrongdoing. That's where the pain was coming from.

"I'm sorry, Irene," Uncle Cecil said at last.

The cry grew into the wail. "You were unfaithful to me?"

Uncle Cecil buried his face in his hands and his voice wasn't quite steady when he said, "It was after you miscarried that last time. We both went through a rough time."

Miscarried? Briana had never heard anything about that. Her aunt and uncle had never had children, but she'd assumed that was by choice. When her aunt began to cry, great wrenching sobs, she wished she were a million miles away.

"I'd never done anything like that before, and I never did again," Uncle Cecil said, moving to sit on the couch beside his wife, who turned her back on him. "I was angry and upset with the world and you weren't yourself. I didn't know what to do or where to turn." He touched the sobbing woman's shoulder, his face twisted with love and remorse.

"I ended up in some dive bar down in Victory Park. I figured nobody knew me down there, and if I wanted to get liquored up and forget my troubles, it was my business.

"I got good and drunk, then left the bar. But I dropped my keys trying to get into the car. A blonde picked them up for me and, well, it was crazy. I was crazy. I never would have done anything if I'd been sober, and if we weren't going through that bad time."

A tear tracked down her uncle's face. "God, I'm sorry Irene. I'd do anything if it weren't true."

Quietly, Briana rose and headed for the door. He *had* done something, Briana thought. He'd tried to destroy the man he believed had dug up the old arrest report and fed it to the media. The man she loved.

She hadn't realized there'd been a bad time in her aunt and uncle's marriage, or that they'd faced the tragedy of wanting children and never having them. That made her sympathetic to their plight, but still, she couldn't forgive Uncle Cecil.

Not yet.

Wouldn't it have been better if he'd been honest with his wife about his horrendous lapse in judgment when it first happened, rather than going to such absurd and unsavory lengths to hush up the truth?

Of course it would.

He'd done wrong. Briana could find it in her heart to forgive him for the first lapse. But as for manipulating her to do his dirty work, just so the truth would stay buried, no, that she was going to find very hard to forgive.

She got into her car with a heavy heart. Her first impulse was to drive to Patrick's place and throw herself in his arms. But a quick check of the clock showed her it was getting on for eleven. His children would be in bed asleep; he might well be asleep, too. He deserved his rest. As always, he had a busy Monday ahead of him.

And so did she.

She had to admit to the man she loved that she was a fraud.

CHAPTER FIFTEEN

BRIANA ARRIVED home tired in mind and body. Because she needed something comforting, she made herself a cup of warm milk, then played back the two new messages on her machine. The first one was Patrick. "Hi, me again. Don't mean to keep bothering you. I just wondered if you were home yet. Call me." The time on that one was 8:00 p.m.

A final message had been left at ten thirty-five. It was Patrick again, sounding edgy. "Look, I'm not a stalker or anything, but I'm getting kind of worried. Is everything okay? Call me whenever you get in. I love you."

She closed her eyes and willed his love to be strong enough to withstand her treachery. She dialed his number. He answered on the first ring.

"Hi," she said, feeling a little breathless just to hear his voice. "It's me. I just got in."

"Thanks for calling. Where have you— No. Sorry. Not my business, I wasn't trying to harass you. But the way things are going in our town, you never know what's going to happen next."

She smiled into the phone. "I think it's sweet that you worried about me. No one's worried about me in a long time."

"I don't only worry about you, I love you. Don't forget that one."

"I'm not going to forget it," she said, feeling marginally better. There were still some good men in the world. "I took a drive up the coast today."

"Lots to think about?"

"Yes. Um..." She had to tell him everything, but not right this minute. It was too raw. And she couldn't tell him on the phone. This had to be done in person. "Could you find some time for me tomorrow?"

"You know I could. Briana, you sound so serious. What's up?"

"I..." She fought the urge to unburden herself right now and get it over with. But it wouldn't be fair to launch into such a seedy story of treachery and deceit over the phone. "I'll tell you all about it tomorrow."

"You're not secretly married to someone else, are you?" He said it in a half-joking way, but she heard the hint of worry in his tone.

Well, at least what she had to tell him wasn't as bad as that. She let herself relax. "No. It has nothing to do with my feelings for you."

"That's a relief, because I happen to think our personal relationship is damn fine. And it's only going to get better."

"I feel so much better for talking to you."

"Me, too. Talk to my admin assistant about scheduling a meeting, will you?"

She laughed. "Will do. Night."

"Night."

To say she slept well would be a gross overstatement, but at least she slept. When she got up the next morning, she made herself some fresh-squeezed orange juice, figuring she needed all the vitamins and energy she could get, and cooked herself oatmeal. Good old-fashioned comfort food. Thus fueled for what she was certain would be a difficult day, she chose a muted outfit of black linen slacks and jacket and a white silk tank, then she was on her way to the office.

She hadn't felt this nervous since she'd arrived for her first day on the job, knowing she was here under false pretenses and feeling miserable about her deceit.

When she arrived, Patrick was already in.

The minute he heard her, he came out of his office. He'd already abandoned his jacket and was in his shirtsleeves. One look at him had her hormones charging into overdrive.

"Hi," he said with a goofy smile on his face.

"Hi," she said back, certain there was an equally goofy smile on her own face.

He stepped forward, and for a second she thought he was going to kiss her right there in the office, but he caught himself and said, "I checked my schedule for today, but it's pretty tight."

"Oh, of course it is. I was forgetting." She pulled it up on her computer as she spoke, and glanced at her watch. "You've got Archie coming in about fifteen minutes, then a budget meeting, then the Courage Bay Pioneer Association lunch." She looked up. "Archie should bring your speaking notes for that when he comes in."

She scanned the rest of the day. "I think I could fit myself into the schedule around eight o'clock tonight," she said.

"I'm sorry, Briana. If it's important, I'll figure out something."

"No." She gave him a forced smile. "It's nothing that important. I'll hang around and do some paperwork, and when you're all done for the day, maybe… Oh, no. What am I thinking? You'll need to get home and see Dylan and Fiona before they go to bed."

"You could come with me," he offered. "Fiona's been dying for you to read that new storybook you bought her. Once they're in bed, we can talk as long as you like." He smiled a little wistfully. "I wish I could offer you more than talk, but…"

"No. Really. I understand. I want to talk to you. The other…" She smiled at him, unable to stop herself. "The other can wait."

"Never mind your paperwork tonight. Go home on time. Update your resume. You're putting in for a transfer."

"Yes. Absolutely." But, she thought, she wouldn't do it until tomorrow. She needed to know that Patrick was still on her side after she told him what she'd done.

BRIANA HAD SAID this meeting wasn't about their personal life, but Patrick didn't like the way she was acting—a little nervous, and having trouble fully meeting his eyes. He'd joked about another man, but she'd laughed and said it wasn't that, and he believed her.

What else could be bothering her so much that she wanted to talk seriously to him the day after they formally became lovers? The day after they'd declared their love?

Archie Weld talked his ear off about the city's communication plan and his update on disaster communications. Since Patrick had become mayor, he'd learned that every disaster involved media relations. It was essential to ensure that information provided to the media was accurate and timely and accessible so that people would stay calm and know what to do.

The city staff in Courage Bay were becoming experts at disaster communication, and he wished it weren't because they'd had so much practice.

He had to cut Archie off to make it to his next appointment on time, and after that, his day was pretty much a dead run from meeting to meeting. He pulled himself together to give his speech at a luncheon for some of Courage Bay's oldest citizens, loading on the praise for the way they'd built this city and helped hold it together.

On the way to his budget planning session, he pulled his tape recorder out of his briefcase and dictated some notes. There were several hundredth birthdays coming up in the city, and he wanted to talk to Archie and Briana about organizing something special.

When he got back to the office at five o'clock, after spending all afternoon on the budget, Briana wasn't there. She'd left the light on and the door unlocked, which could indicate she was returning, or maybe she'd simply forgotten. Probably she'd forgotten to close up properly in her haste to get working on that resume, he thought with a smug smile.

He was pleased she'd followed his orders and gone home, although he could still smell a lingering hint of her scent.

He didn't want to rush the woman, but he had "for richer, for poorer, till death do us part" on his mind.

A few minutes remained before he had to leave for a dinner meeting, so he called home and chatted to both his kids. They sounded happy, fed and reasonably well-entertained with a Disney video, and he promised he'd be home in time to tuck them in.

With the phone still in his hand, he contemplated calling Briana at home, but after he'd hounded her shamelessly all day Sunday, and he'd already seen her in the office this morning, he thought calling her might be too much.

She'd left his correspondence for the day, ready to be signed and mailed. He scanned each item briefly and then signed it. Since she wasn't in, he even stuck the things in the envelopes.

As he pulled his notes from the earlier meeting out of his briefcase, a glint of silver caught his eye. Right. He'd dictated some notes earlier that needed typing up.

The tape was pretty far advanced. He couldn't remember what was on the first part, so he pressed Rewind, and then Play.

For a few seconds there was blank tape. Then some muffled sounds like someone fumbling around in a sock drawer. He must have left the machine on by mistake at some point. He was about to push Fast Forward when he heard Briana's voice, as though she were talking from inside a sleeping bag, the words inaudible but the voice recognizably hers.

Then he heard his voice. "I want you so much, Briana. I want to make love with you."

There was more shuffling and then Briana's voice. "Are you taking off my blouse?"

A low chuckle answered her. "I'm trying, but damn it I'm out of practice."

Patrick heard the passion in his voice, and in that second was transported back to that dark elevator, where heaven had seemed in his grasp.

He was stunned and laid the recorder on the desk, letting the tape continue. He knew what he was hearing, the entire encounter in the elevator the first time they'd made love. Now he recalled that the elevator repair guy had given him the recorder the following morning, so it must somehow have fallen out of his briefcase and turned itself on.

Then off? Why hadn't the tape kept going to the end?

The funny thing was that he hadn't recalled having the recorder with him the night they'd been trapped in the elevator. Usually, he kept it in the glove compartment of his car.

Probably, he was crazy. But he had a bad feeling in his belly. On a hunch, he ran downstairs and out to his car. He unlocked and opened the passenger side door and reached in. He felt as if he was moving in slow motion as he clicked open the glove compartment.

His tape recorder was there. Right where he'd left it. He picked it up and took it with him back to his office.

When he compared it to the other one, he saw they were almost identical. Same make, same model. One looked a little newer. The one with a recording of him and Briana on it.

He played the sex-in-the-elevator tape again. And this time, he got a sick sense of why she was asking him what he was doing. It hadn't been for the erotic thrill of describing to each other what they were doing in the dark. She'd wanted to get what they were doing on tape.

But why?

Patrick returned to that night in his mind. It was easy enough, since he recalled every second and had relived it in memory many times.

For some reason, she'd had a tape recorder in her bag when the pair of them got on that elevator.

Could she have pushed the record button by accident?

He closed his eyes, forcing his memory to stay sharp even as unease churned in his gut.

She'd gone into her purse for condoms, he recalled, and then again for her phone. But this had been activated much earlier. The recording began when he'd started to undress her.

Once more he picked up the tape recorder and inspected it. The On button was slightly depressed—all the controls were, presumably to avoid the thing being activated accidentally. She hadn't even been holding her bag when he'd started removing her blouse. It had been on the floor somewhere beside them.

It seemed likely that she'd reached into her bag at some point and pushed the button to record. Okay, he told himself, maybe she was a woman who liked to record her own sexual encounters. It was a little on the kinky side, but only mildly so. He agreed that it was a turn-on to listen to them, or it would be if he weren't fighting this feeling of disquiet.

His uneasiness only increased as he acknowledged that when she'd told him she had a cell phone in her bag the night of the aftershock, he'd been surprised she hadn't mentioned it earlier. She'd explained that she didn't believe it would work when the regular phones were down, but she was such an intelligent woman, he'd decided the shock must have made her temporarily confused. Now he wondered.

Had she known all along that her phone would work just fine? But she wouldn't have wanted help to arrive, not if she were deliberately trying to seduce him.

Oh, that was ridiculous, he thought, rising and pacing around the small outer office. He wasn't the president of the United States, he was a small-town mayor. What possible motive could she have to tape his sexual advances?

It was as ridiculous as her suggesting to him that the story and photograph that destroyed Cecil Thomson's mayoralty campaign were fake.

He turned the recorder off, right when things were at their peak in that elevator. He wanted that moment to remain a good memory for him. Damn, he hoped there was an innocent explanation for why one of the most incredible, intimate experiences of his life was on tape.

Patrick wasn't a big believer in conspiracy theories, but he was unsettled enough to think maybe it wouldn't be a bad idea to do some checking up on Briana Bliss. Just so he could find out she was the woman he'd believed her to be when he'd fallen in love with her. Just to put his mind at rest.

Walking back into his office, he went straight for his computer and accessed the employment records. Briana Bliss. There she was. And there was her social security number. Five minutes and a few keystrokes later, he had her mother's maiden name.

Thomson.

Of course, there were thousands, possibly millions of Thomsons in the States. It could be pure coincidence that Briana's mother's birth name happened to be the same as the only man in Courage Bay who hated Patrick.

But Patrick had been a politician long enough to know that people weren't always what they seemed, and not to trust coincidences. He also knew that some part of him would never recover if his newly healed heart was broken a second time, this time not through tragedy but deliberate betrayal.

In retrospect, he wished his computer skills weren't so

good, or the system was slower. With some computer savvy and a social security number, it was amazing how much you could find out about a person. He had his answer before he'd had time to prepare for the worst.

Briana's mother was the sister of Cecil Thomson. Which made the man who was clearly his enemy and political rival the uncle of his admin assistant.

Patrick sat back and stared at his computer screen, his fingers steepled in front of his mouth as he worked out the details of the trap he'd fallen into.

Cecil Thomson had wanted the mayor's job.

Cecil Thomson didn't get a majority vote because of an unsavory incident from his past, and the people of Courage Bay had had it with sexual misconduct from their civic leaders.

Sexual misconduct had caused one mayor to be booted out of office and a contender to lose his chance. If Mayor Patrick O'Shea, whose victory was based on his ethics and morality, could be caught in sexual misconduct, then he'd be history, and the chances were good that the people of Courage Bay would look at Cecil Thomson with a kinder eye.

It was such a perfect setup, Patrick almost admired the wiles that had caused Thomson to insinuate his beautiful niece into Patrick's office and let nature take its course. If she could entrap him into sexual harassment, and provide the kind of proof the media loved, then Patrick's career would be destroyed. Cecil Thomson would have another shot at running for mayor.

Resisting the impulse to throw back his head and howl like a wounded wolf, Patrick forced himself to consider his situation with cold reason. And what he saw didn't impress him.

The biggest irony was that if Patrick had held on to the high standards he'd believed himself to possess, the plot would have failed. But he hadn't counted on falling in love with the woman who was his assistant.

Briana. He moaned her name inside his head. What possible reason could she have for such betrayal?

He was going to find out. Knowing he would be incapable of acting rationally tonight, he called and canceled his evening meeting.

Then he returned, with the tape recorder, to Briana's desk, feeling about a hundred years older than he had an hour ago, and with a bitter taste in his mouth and bleak anger in his heart.

He sat down in her chair and tried to imagine how it had felt to be her, to make love with a man for the sole purpose of destroying his life, and he found he couldn't. It seemed as though he was going to have a chance to ask her, though, because he heard her voice talking to someone in the hall.

She hadn't gone home, after all. Soon she was going to wish she had.

CHAPTER SIXTEEN

"DON'T WORK TOO LATE," Briana said as she turned toward the mayor's office and the land titles clerk continued down the corridor.

"You either," the clerk called back to her.

In truth, Briana wasn't here for work. She'd decided to wait until Patrick returned so she could tell him what she'd done; she wanted to do it in the office setting and not in his home. Somehow that seemed important. It was only as his admin assistant that she'd been a fraud. Never, from the first moment they'd kissed, she realized now, had it been an option for her to go through with what Uncle Cecil had planned.

It was in the office that she'd been untruthful, and it was in the office that she would explain why. She wouldn't pollute Patrick's home, the home he shared with Dylan and Fiona, with the unsavory tale.

She walked into the office and stopped on the threshold, her heart jumping in her throat—first with gladness, when she saw Patrick sitting in her chair with his feet up on her desk, then with a sick foreboding when she recognized the object he held in his hand.

The tape recorder. And in it the tape, she'd made of them

in the elevator. That wretched, stupid tape that had gone missing after their night together.

Any possibility that he didn't know what was recorded in that small box was put to rest when she saw the expression on his face. His lips were clenched so tight it was amazing they didn't crack. More than anger blazed coldly out of those searing blue eyes. There was contempt, too.

Her face flamed and she couldn't hold his gaze.

"Patrick, I—" She what? Could she possibly make him believe there was an explanation that was innocent? Even as she considered trying to dredge one up, she knew she wouldn't. She was done with lies and dishonesty. This man deserved the truth.

Instead of saying a single world, instead of yelling at her, berating her, all of which she deserved, he picked up the recorder and pushed Play.

"No," she pleaded softly. "Please, don't."

But already the room was filled with the sounds of panting, the rustle of clothing, the sigh of flesh against flesh and a soft guttural cry that she knew must be hers, since it was distinctly female. Oh, and that female was having the time of her life.

"Oh, Briana, you feel so good," Patrick said on tape, his voice hoarse with passion.

"Yes," she cried. "Oh, oh, yes…" Her cheeks flamed, and Briana could take no more. Stepping swiftly forward, she grabbed the recorder out of his hand and pushed Stop.

She'd wanted the mechanical replay of that wonderful night to end, but now the dead silence seemed almost as bad. She put the recorder onto the desk with a soft click and stepped back. She'd wanted to tell him everything, but of course, she'd never in all her life intended to tell him about the tape. There'd have been no need if she could have destroyed it the following day, as she'd intended to.

Now, here it was, damning her before she'd had a chance to explain.

Her throat felt dry, so dry, and all the explanations she knew Patrick deserved and that she wanted to give him wouldn't come to her.

When she didn't speak, he did.

"So you wanted to set me up for a sexual harassment suit." He put his hand on the recorder and pushed it toward her. "Go ahead. Call your lawyer."

She glanced up, startled. "No."

"You'll need a lawyer anyway. You're fired." He laughed without mirth. "It's pretty ironic, isn't it? I wanted so desperately for you not to work for me anymore. I begged you to transfer, I had my eye open for challenging positions so you could get a well-deserved promotion. And when you, with all your talent and experience, wouldn't take a transfer, I put it down to your loyalty."

"Patrick, please."

"I finally have a good reason to fire you. Sue me, do whatever the hell you want. Maybe you'll even get *your uncle Cecil* my job after all. He sure wants it badly enough." He stopped, and she saw the depth of his pain in the hard pewter of his eyes. "The only thing I can't figure out is what was in it for you?"

"Nothing," she said. She raised a hand toward him and he stared at her as though she were vermin.

"Nothing? Oh, honey, there has to be something you wanted bad. Is it tabloid fame? Maybe the three of us—

you, me and Uncle Cecil—can go on one of those afternoon talk shows where everybody betrays everybody else and they yell and beat up on each other on national television. Is that what you're after?"

"No. Look, I told you I wanted to talk to you tonight. I was going to tell you everything."

"I'll just bet you were."

"I wish you'd listen to me."

Patrick looked at her, and the lines of anger couldn't hide the pain and loss in his eyes. "I really don't think I want to. You and your uncle proved your point. I was corruptible."

"No!" she cried, desperate to make him listen to her. "That's not true."

"I thought because I loved you that it changed the rules somehow." He shook his head so stiffly it looked like his neck hurt. "The rules don't work that way. What I did was wrong, and against my principles." He snorted. "Some white knight I turned out to be." He rose. "Take the tape and have your fun. Do your best to bring me down and see how much you enjoy it."

He picked up the tape recorder and pushed it toward her.

She shoved her hands behind her back. "No. I don't want it."

"Take it. It's your property. If there's anything else here that belongs to you personally, you can take that, too, then I'll need your keys back. I'll be escorting you off the premises."

"I tried to find the tape the next morning so I could destroy it. I never, ever would have used it. You must know that. I believed—" She bit her lip. "My uncle and aunt were so good to me. I owe them so much. I—well, I can't talk about that part. I got my loyalties mixed up."

"Why couldn't you tell me what was going on? You had plenty of opportunity Saturday night," he reminded her.

"I showed you the newspaper article, remember?"

He nodded curtly.

"I believed someone had fabricated that story about my uncle. Yesterday, I went to see the officer who originally made the arrest." She shook her head. "You weren't the only one who was betrayed," she said sadly.

"I'm all out of pity. Let's go."

Briana couldn't believe this was happening. It was a nightmare. She was being fired from the job she loved by the man she'd come to love. Oh, she'd made a big mistake, too. She'd been loyal, as loyal as she knew how to be. But to the wrong man.

There was no possible way she could explain her error to this angry, implacable man. She saw now that she didn't deserve him, anyway. Not after what she'd done. Talk about going against your own principles.

Sadly, she took the tape recorder and placed it in her bag. The only personal items she wanted to take home were the pictures Dylan had drawn for her, but knowing how Patrick must feel about her right now, she doubted he'd want her even to touch his son's artwork. She had her dragon hanging at home on her fridge. At least she could take that one with her as a bittersweet reminder of all she'd lost. Correction—all she'd thrown away.

"There's nothing," she said sadly, and turned for the door. "I'm sorry," she whispered. "I'm just so sorry." She wouldn't cry. Not here and not now. Later. When she was home, she was going on the crying jag to end all crying jags. Until then, she'd hold it together.

A hand grabbed her shoulder before she made it to the door.

"Why?" he demanded, as though he couldn't help himself. "I need to know why."

"I can't explain," she said, and it was true. Even now, she couldn't bring herself to expose her uncle. She still felt the heavy burden of gratitude for what he and her aunt had done for her. And maybe a little pity for the pain Uncle Cecil must have been suffering when he strayed. And what Patrick had said earlier was true for her, as well. If she were the woman of high character she'd believed herself to be, she never would have agreed to take on such an unsavory task. She'd been a fool, but she'd been a dishonest fool, and for that she'd pay a heavy price. "I'm sorry."

And she left. She had no idea whether he followed her or not, because she walked so fast she verged on a trot, down the wide stairs, across the marble foyer, out the double doors and to the parking area. And she never looked back.

Not until she was home.

Then she kicked off her shoes, and before so much as taking off her jacket, she went and got her toolbox. It was pretty much an apartment-dwelling single woman toolbox, with one of those screwdrivers that had about a hundred changeable heads, a pair of pliers and a hammer.

It was the hammer she wanted.

Panting with anger, despair and chagrin, she grabbed the tape recorder out of her bag and marched back outside to the asphalt drive. She flicked the tape out of the recorder and placed it on the ground, then she hammered it, again and again, until the plastic covering was shattered and the shiny brown tape that spilled in messy coils was twisted and mashed and had dirt embedded in it.

Tears were running down her face, and she was sobbing so hard she was having trouble breathing, but she wasn't finished yet. She took the hammer to the metal recorder next and bashed away at that until it looked as though it had been melted in a fire. Not content, she pounded at it until it broke into little pieces.

She swept everything up and put the whole mess in the garbage. She wasn't finished with the tape, though. She went back inside for a pair of shears and cut the tape into little pieces. She then found an old metal pail and went back out with her barbecue lighter and burned as much as she could, not worrying about the toxic smoke. Only then did she drop the whole mess, pail and all, into the garbage.

Then she went back inside, locked the doors, stomped into her bedroom, threw herself fully clothed onto the bed, and sobbed.

The phone rang at some point while she was immersed in grief and self-loathing, but she ignored it. Later, she padded out to the kitchen for a glass of water and played back her voice mail. The call had been from her Uncle Cecil. He'd sounded old and sad and he'd apologized.

She erased the message and then pulled the plug on her phone. She turned away, and as she did, her gaze alighted on the picture Dylan had drawn of the dragon.

Tears leaked out of her all over again as she stared at the drawing that had made her so happy, and now made her so sad.

She managed to brush her teeth and get into her nightclothes and that was it. The rest of the night was spent torturing herself with the knowledge of how much she'd hurt Patrick and his children.

Although she didn't sleep at all, the next morning she felt calmer and able to make a decision.

She was leaving Courage Bay as soon as possible.

She brewed herself some coffee, padding around in her bare feet and cataloguing everything she had to do. It wasn't much. Her rent was paid until the end of the month. She'd call the landlord and pay an extra month's rent in lieu of notice. Since she hadn't even brought a lot of stuff with her, she could pack, clean the place, have her utilities cut off and be on the road before nightfall.

She didn't even know where she was going, and she didn't much care.

Somewhere she'd find another job, and another home, and she'd start all over again. Yes, she thought with a sniff, she'd leave Courage Bay—and her heart—behind her.

PATRICK MADE IT HOME in time to tuck his kids into bed and read Fiona a story. When he recalled his earlier foolish hope that Briana would be here to read Fiona her new storybook, he felt his heart break all over again. This time not for himself, but for Fiona and Dylan, who'd latched on to Briana with the same naive hopes he'd so blithely held.

He wanted to break something, to rail and rant and throw things.

How could any woman be so calculating? So damned uncaring that she'd hurt not only the man who loved her but two innocent children who were also starting to care for her? And how could he have been such a fool?

After the kids were asleep, he helped himself to a rare Scotch and sat in the dark living room staring out the window. If the children weren't in the house, he'd probably drink the entire bottle of Glenfiddich. He smiled wryly. At least his kids were preventing him from a nasty hangover in the morning.

They'd do something else for him, too. They'd pull him through this. They'd got through Janie's death, the three of them, and they could sure as hell get over the defection of a calculating manipulative woman who'd set out to destroy his career.

He thought about that, too, while he sipped the fiery liquid and stared out into the night. His precious career. He'd probably lose it, once Briana and her uncle went public with that tape. There'd be some tough times ahead. He was furious again, with Briana and with himself, that his children would suffer for his indiscretion. Not Fiona so much. She and her friends were too young to understand. But Dylan would have a hard time at school.

He rubbed his face in his hands. He'd never been a quitter, but for the sake of his children, maybe he should make a new start, move somewhere different. He'd paid off the house with Janie's life insurance money and he had some savings. They'd be fine. He could make a new start for his family, find a new job, a new home with no memories.

And yet, good things had happened in this house, as well as bad. His family was here. O'Sheas had lived in Courage Bay for over a hundred years. He'd been a fool and he'd face up to that. But was he going to run away?

Hell, no.

On that determined note, he went to bed, though he really wondered why he bothered. His hurt was too fresh, his anger too raw, so he tossed and turned and finally got up and wrote a speech. Yet another passionate Mayor Patrick O'Shea goes to the people appeal, only this one was more in the line of crisis management.

Damage control, Archie would call it.

When the first few streaks of dawn lit the sky, he decided to call it morning and got into the shower. By the time Mrs. Simpson arrived at seven-thirty, he'd gone through the better part of two pots of coffee, had read the paper cover to cover, and written Briana a letter. Two, in fact. He'd torn up both of them, but he felt better for expressing some of the hurt and anger and disbelief that raged within him.

He dressed carefully, and when he left the house, he was already preparing himself for one of the toughest days of his career.

Of his life.

There were no TV crews or reporters outside his house, for which he silently thanked the brass at the local media. This was Courage Bay, California, and the media would hound him at work rather than waylay him at home, where his kids would be upset.

It was one reason he'd be at his desk on time and accessible to any reporter who wanted him. He wouldn't hide what he'd done. He was ashamed of his actions and he'd apologize. The rest, he supposed, was up to the people of the community.

He accepted that he might end up turfed out of his job, but he was going to do everything he could to lobby for someone decent to take over as mayor. Cecil Thomson and his heartless niece may have succeeded in destroying Patrick's career, but they were going to discover it was a hollow victory. Cecil was never going to be mayor if Patrick could help it. He'd use every means at his disposal—every honest and ethical means—to make sure someone of decency and character held the mayor's office.

Courage Bay deserved a good mayor. It had certainly had a string of lousy ones.

Gritting his teeth, he prepared for a media scrum when he reached city hall, but there was nothing out of the ordinary going on. He'd called Archie at home and requested a meeting first thing.

When Patrick got to his office, he was surprised for a second that the door was still locked. Grimly, he opened up and flipped on the lights himself.

When Archie arrived for their meeting, his first words were, "Where's Briana?"

"I fired her."

"What?" The man was so stunned he dropped his pen on the ground. "It's not April Fools' Day already, is it?"

"No." Patrick sighed heavily. "You'd better sit down. You're not going to like what I have to say." And Patrick told his media manager the truth. All of it.

Archie didn't say anything for a minute, but his face registered stunned disbelief. Then he blew out a breath. "Wow."

"I'm sorry, Archie. I'm apologizing to you, and as soon as you think it's right, I'm apologizing to the people of Courage Bay. I screwed up."

"Whoa, there. I appreciate the apology, and there is no question that you screwed up, but let's not go rushing out for a public whipping quite yet." Archie leaned back and began tapping his pen against his binder.

"Archie, if you're planning something, forget it. I did wrong. I'm not going to hide."

Archie glanced at Patrick with eyes that weren't nearly as condemning as he thought he deserved. "Patrick, I said you screwed up, and it's true, you did. But you're still a good man and the best hope Courage Bay has as a mayor. Should you have slept with your assistant? Hell, no. But I'm not going to pretend I didn't notice there was more than professional respect between the two of you. You handled it quietly, you're both single. I was ready to step in with a word if I'd suspected a problem."

He tapped his pen against his binder again in a way that was getting on Patrick's nerves. "You and Briana having a quiet romance wouldn't be that big a deal. Briana setting you up for sexual harassment, however..."

The communications manager shook his head. "I'm obviously not as shocked as you are, but I'm beyond surprised. I would have pegged Briana Bliss as almost as decent, God-fearing and loyal as you are yourself."

"Well, I guess she fooled us both."

"More than the two of us. Everybody liked Briana. Hell, this is awful."

"Tell me about it."

"Okay, first thing I'm going to do is get you a temp for today."

Patrick nodded.

"You shouldn't have let her take that tape, buddy," Archie said.

"I guess not," Patrick admitted. "I was so angry I wasn't thinking straight."

Archie tapped some more. Patrick bit his tongue. He needed someone on his side, and he was relieved that his media manager was willing to be that someone. "Strange she hasn't gone public with that tape," Archie said. "I wonder why? Cecil will use it to divert attention from the funding crisis, of course." He shrugged. "Right now, you're still a hero and he's one of the most unpopular men in Courage Bay. If I was his media advisor, I'd tell him to get that tape out today."

"It's a good thing you're on my side, and not his."

"Don't worry." Archie grinned. "I'll do everything I can to keep Cecil Thomson out of that chair," he said, pointing to the one Patrick was currently sitting in, "and you in it."

Patrick nodded. He was pleased to hear he still had Archie's support even after his admission. "Me, too. I'm not sure that's possible, though."

"It all depends on Briana, I guess. I'm going to call up a couple of old friends in radio and at the paper. If there's any hint of anything coming down the pipe, they'll tell me."

Patrick rose and stretched. His limbs felt stiff, as though he'd been beaten. "I'm telling you again, Archie, I'm not hiding from this."

"I hear you, but don't do anything public without my say so. Agreed?"

He nodded shortly. "Agreed."

Within the hour, he had a perky young temp he'd seen in the building before. Her name was Lucy and she had twin daughters a year behind Dylan at school. Lucy was pleasant on the phone, knew how to use the computer and showed absolutely no initiative.

He ached every time he walked by her desk and realized Briana was gone. And why.

Fortunately, he had nothing scheduled that couldn't be rescheduled and Archie took care of that, insisting Patrick stay around until they knew what damage control would be required. He'd advised Patrick not to tell anyone that Briana was fired. She was off for the day and that's all the information they were giving out. Tomorrow was soon enough for the paperwork and the lawyers.

So Patrick found himself in the office, stuck at his desk trying to work. But his mind felt foggy.

He'd told Lucy he was busy with important paperwork and not to be disturbed, then he closed his door.

About eleven-thirty, his office door flew open. He glanced up from staring blankly at a report, expecting to see Archie holding back a pack of baying reporters. Instead he saw his sister, Shannon, standing there. He was so surprised he blinked hard, as though she were an apparition.

"You should tell the temps there's no point trying to keep me out," she said, breezing in wearing full uniform. No, Patrick thought, no apparition would talk to him that way. "I was in the neighborhood and came to drag you off for lunch. Where's…" Her words petered out when she saw Patrick's face.

"My God, Patrick, what happened?" she asked in an entirely different tone. "You look like you did the day Janie died."

Patrick rose from his desk and stalked to the window. "Nothing so tragic." He stared out at the street below, wondering how much to tell his sister. Then he decided, the hell with it. The world would know soon enough. She might as well be among the first.

He turned back to her. "Briana isn't the woman I thought she was."

"What exactly does that mean?"

"It means I fired her." He told Shannon everything. About the tape, the confrontation, his plans to come clean. "Archie made me promise we'd wait and let them strike first."

"Archie's a smart guy, and you're not firing on all cylinders today. Listen to him, bro." She stood there, so serious in her navy uniform, a frown gathering on her face. "I can't believe this," she said finally. "I absolutely cannot believe it. Briana was in love with you. I'd bet my life on it."

"I've had all night to get used to the fact that she's a good actress. I think I'll take a rain check on lunch, if you don't mind."

She nodded. "I've lost my appetite, too."

CHAPTER SEVENTEEN

"SO, YOU BREAK my brother's heart, now you're running away. You really are a piece of work." Shannon O'Shea was the last person Briana had expected to see on her doorstep. The woman eyed the packing boxes in the hall as though she'd like to kick them. After their conversation at Dylan's birthday party about how Shannon would take Briana apart if she ever hurt Patrick, maybe she should have expected the tough-talking firefighter to show up at her door with vengeance sparking from her eyes.

"Have you come to beat me up?" Briana asked. She was so deep in misery she didn't care. A little physical pain might help relieve the inner ache. Of course, Shannon knew of Briana's treachery. Everyone in the city probably knew about it by now. "I know I deserve to be beaten up. Go ahead."

Her eyes were red-rimmed from crying, her cheeks chapped. She'd never been a pretty crier. Even her hair seemed depressed. It hung lank around her face since she hadn't bothered to do anything with it once she'd got out of the shower. What was the point?

"Don't tempt me. I'd like to smack you from here to tomorrow. I just left my brother looking almost as bad as he did the day they buried his wife." Shannon stepped over a half-packed box and glared. "How could you do this to him?"

Briana had believed she was all cried out, but discovered there was a fresh supply of tears just waiting to flood her cheeks.

"I couldn't," she sobbed. "I believed he'd leaked that story about my uncle Cecil and the prostitute that ran in the paper, the one that cost Uncle Cecil the election and allowed Patrick to win." She stopped to blow her nose on a tissue she'd stuffed in her pocket. It was already tear-damp. "But he didn't. He—he wasn't even the one who l-leaked the story to the paper."

"Of course he wasn't. What were you thinking?" Shannon yelled at her. "My brother is the most honest, uncomplicated man there ever was. He had to be bullied into running for mayor." She stomped farther inside and slammed the front door behind her. "Believe me, he'd have been relieved if he'd lost the election."

"Okay, so I know that now. I didn't at the time."

"I heard Patrick's version of the story. Now I'd like to hear yours."

"Patrick wouldn't listen." She wiped her wet face with the back of her hand. "I was going to tell him last night. I planned to tell him everything." She shook her head. "No. That's not true. I was never going to tell him about the tape. I was going to destroy it. Except I lost it. Remember when I phoned you to see if you'd found anything in the elevator? I made up some lame excuse about a missing earring, but it was the tape I wanted. So I could destroy it."

Briana grabbed a fresh tissue. "Would you like some coffee?"

"Yeah."

So the two of them sat in the kitchen and drank coffee. Because she was such an emotional wreck, Briana wasn't the most efficient packer today. There were plates piled on the counter, but she hadn't boxed them yet. Cutlery was in a silver heap by the sink. Some things she couldn't decide whether to keep or chuck were sitting on the counter beside the fridge. And blazing down at her from its prized spot on the refrigerator door was the picture Dylan had drawn for her. She cried anew every time she glimpsed it, but she wouldn't take it down. She deserved the punishment.

"Sorry about the mess. I need to get more boxes." Except she couldn't make herself go out to get them. She thought people might hiss at her and throw rotten eggs and tomatoes.

Taking a sip of coffee, she told Shannon the truth. All of it. "I was wrong. What I did was terrible." A tear dripped into her coffee, rippling the surface. Usually she added milk, but today black suited her mood.

"What did you do with the tape?" Shannon asked. She'd listened in silence to the story and now stared at Briana with an implacable expression.

"It's in a million pieces in the garbage can."

"A million pieces?"

Briana nodded. "First I mashed it with a hammer, then I cut the tape up with scissors." She sniffed. "Then I burned it."

"I see."

"I thought it might make me feel better. But it didn't. At least no one will ever be able to play that tape."

"Patrick's sitting in his office expecting a media scrum any minute. He thinks you're still out to destroy him."

"No!" She leaped to her feet, knocking the table so the coffee sloshed in their cups and slopped over the sides. "How can he believe that? I told him I would never use that tape. Why didn't he believe me?"

"I leave that to you to decide," Shannon said. "He told me he won't hide from the truth. He's all ready to make a public confession."

"But, we have to stop him. He'll hurt his career if he does that."

"He thinks you're trying to kill his career, you and your uncle."

She shook her head. "Please, will you tell him no one will ever know about us?" She sniffed dismally at the thought. "And tell him I destroyed that stupid tape. I would never have used it against him anyway. I couldn't."

"I don't think Patrick would believe anything you told him. Not sure I do, either."

Briana dug into the pocket of her old jeans and pulled out a piece of metal. She handed it to Shannon.

"What is this? It looks like shrapnel."

"It's part of the tape recorder. I found it in the driveway this morning."

Shannon's eyebrows rose. "You sure did a number on that thing."

"I made a terrible mistake. I'm sorry."

"Well, sister," Shannon said, dropping the twisted piece of metal to the table with a clink, "sorry isn't going to cut it. What do you plan to do about your mistake?"

Shannon was an imposing woman at the best of times, but in uniform, and standing at her full height of close to six feet, she was downright intimidating.

"I'm leaving the city. I'll start over somewhere new." She almost choked on the words, realizing, now that it was too late, how much she'd come to love Courage Bay and feel at home.

"Like I figured. You're running away."

"Do you think you could leave me a little pride?" Briana was crying openly again, the tears running down her face faster than she could wipe them away.

"Nope." Shannon passed her a half-empty box of tissues from the kitchen counter.

"Did you come to gloat?"

"No. I came to make sure you do the right thing."

"I'm doing the best I can," Briana sniffed. "I'm leaving. Patrick can forget about me and move on with his life."

"And what about his kids? What about Dylan and Fiona?" Shannon asked.

Even hearing their names had Briana's misery increasing. Oh, she was going to miss them. How could she not have noticed that she'd fallen in love with them, too?

"My leaving is the best thing for them. They'll get over me."

"I told you before, I only care about my family. And you are not going anywhere before you say goodbye to those kids."

"But Patrick would—"

"The hell with Patrick. He's not thinking any straighter than you are. Dylan and Fiona already had one woman they loved leave them without saying goodbye. Did you ever think of that? Instead of whining and sniveling over yourself, maybe you could think about how those kids are going to feel if they never see you again and never understand why. Do you think that's good for them?"

Briana shook her head, her misery so deep she'd lost the ability to think. Shannon was right, though. How selfish of her not to realize she owed those children a proper goodbye.

"Okay. You're right. I'll go and see them." She gestured vaguely around her. "Just as soon as I finish packing."

"The kids'll be home from school by now. I'll take you."

Briana gaped.

"Come on. I've got to get back to the station house. I don't have all day."

"I can drive myself."

"Quit arguing and come on."

Since Shannon was fitter, stronger and bigger than she was, Briana didn't have much choice but to obey. It was best to get this over with anyway.

She shoved her feet into sneakers and they walked outside. Briana blinked.

"You came here in an official fire department vehicle?"

"Be glad it's not a police cruiser or you'd be in the back wearing cuffs."

LUCY BROUGHT Patrick a sandwich and put it on his desk without even being asked. Okay, so maybe she did show some initiative. Because he didn't want to act as churlish as he felt, he thanked her and ate it. He couldn't have said afterward what the filling was.

He went back to pretending to work, and his next visitor was the last one he'd have expected, and the least welcome.

His intercom buzzed.

"Councilman Thomson is here to see you," Lucy said.

"Tell him—" Patrick stopped before he could claim he was too busy. Thomson wanted to gloat about the tape? Fine. Patrick had a few words he'd like to say to that slimeball himself. "Tell him to come in."

He rose so he was standing at his full height behind his imposing desk when the councilman walked in.

Patrick didn't even make a pretense of offering to shake hands, and Thomson didn't, either. Even knowing there was a blood relationship between this man and Briana, Patrick was hard-pressed to see it. They both had green eyes, and that was it for any physical resemblance. But it seemed Cecil Thomson and Briana Bliss's characters were more similar than their looks, as he'd discovered at his cost.

"What do you want?" Patrick asked coldly.

Thomson looked gray, and his hand shook as he produced a paper from his briefcase and placed it on Patrick's desk. "It's my vote for the approval of expenditure of public funds for emergency services."

"What?" Patrick could barely believe his ears. He'd expected a gloating Thomson had come to blackmail him into resigning, which of course he wouldn't have countenanced. He'd planned to go down fighting.

Patrick snatched up the document to read it, and found it was indeed an approval for the release of the emergency funding.

"Why are you doing this?"

"I'm not a man for apologies, but it seems I wronged you. I'm trying to make it up."

Patrick put the paper back on his desk. "You wronged me, all right. You think this is going to make everything fine?" His anger roared back. This was probably some trick, and as soon as the funding was announced, Thomson would leak that damn tape. Patrick wondered if that would be his punishment. He'd get the funding, but it would be Thomson of all people who'd administer it. Well, getting the funding was the right thing to do, and if losing his job was the price he had to pay to get it, he supposed he'd pay.

"No." The older man sighed heavily and sank into one of Patrick's visitor chairs, though he hadn't been invited. He reached into his briefcase and pulled out another document. "My resignation."

"You're resigning from council so you'll have more time to run for mayor?" Patrick asked.

Thomson looked up at him and he saw the older man's eyes were red-rimmed and baggy. He looked old and defeated.

Thomson shook his head. "I'm done with politics. I'm taking my wife away for a vacation and we're going to try to heal our marriage. I wronged her, and then made a worse mess of things by trying to cover up. I've lost my niece because of it." He stopped for a moment, and to Patrick's horror, he realized the man was fighting tears. "I won't let my wife give up on me."

"You lost your niece?" Patrick felt like he was missing something important here.

"I never should have asked her to help me take you down. I never would have if I hadn't believed you and your buddy Max Zirinsky had leaked that old police arrest to the media. My wife was badly hurt by it and I wanted to blame somebody other than myself. Turns out I was wrong. Briana was convinced you hadn't done it. She told me you were always doing the right thing, and you never laid a hand on her or acted with any impropriety."

Briana had told him that? She'd lied again, but this time to protect Patrick's reputation, not destroy it, or so it seemed. But he was so befuddled and confused he wasn't even sure he was hearing right.

"So my niece started digging to find out who'd planted those lies. I told her and my wife the whole thing was faked. Briana lov—" Thomson's voice wobbled with emotion and he stopped until he'd regained control. "She believed in me. She was grateful because we'd paid for her schooling and some other things. She gave me her loyalty."

Patrick was still furious Briana had done what she'd done, but he could almost understand that kind of blind loyalty. There was a lot of it in his family.

"Well, she found out you'd had nothing to do with leaking the story, and she found out the incident really had happened and that I'd lied to her and my wife about it. She came to visit me last night and—" Once more he had to stop and regain control. "Well, she nailed me. Now my wife knows that I strayed badly all those years ago. I hope she can forgive me one day."

"What did Briana say when she came over?" Patrick didn't have a lot of pity for Thomson, and he was determined to hear all of it.

"Well, you must know. She said she was going to tell you everything. About what I'd done, and how she'd come here under false pretenses."

"She didn't get the opportunity," Patrick said, wishing now that he'd at least given her a chance. But he'd been so blindsided, so angry. So hurt.

"My only consolation is that my plan failed. You didn't attempt to compromise Briana in any way, so no harm done. Now I've got things in better perspective, I'm hoping to save my marriage and one day repair the rift with Briana. I'm finished with politics."

Oh, no. Thomson was so wrong about the harm he'd caused. There had been harm. Patrick and Briana had suffered. Although Patrick was having a hard time sustaining his anger when it was clear that Thomson was being well-punished for his misconduct and lies.

"There's a new gal out front," Thomson said. "Briana quit her job, I suppose? Probably doesn't want to work in a place where she'll have to see me. Tell her I've resigned from council, will you? Maybe she'll reconsider the job."

"I don't think she will," Patrick said. One thing he was determined about. Briana Bliss was never going to be working for him again.

CHAPTER EIGHTEEN

THEY WERE PLAYING in the backyard. Briana heard Dylan's voice, and then Fiona's laughter. It took everything she had not to start crying again.

"Come on." Shannon pretty much frog-marched her through the house, where they exchanged a hurried greeting with the housekeeper, and then Briana was hustled out to the backyard.

Fiona was holding a big red and yellow plastic baseball bat, chubby legs half-bent, her concentration focused on her brother, who held a red plastic baseball ready to pitch.

"Hi, Dylan. Hi, Fiona," she called, forcing herself to sound cheerful.

"Briana!" Fiona cried, and ran over for a hug. Briana squeezed the little girl tight in her arms, loving the healthy child scent of her, the fresh air and peanut-butter sandwich and cherry-scented shampoo smell.

How could she have been so foolish?

Glancing around, she noticed that Shannon had slipped back into the house and she was alone with the kids. "You are so special," she whispered into Fiona's ear, loving the way the clustered curls tickled her nose.

"Wanna play catcher?" Dylan asked. He'd come within

hugging distance, but he was ten now and not inclined to throw himself into her arms, even though she could tell he wanted to.

She hoped Shannon hadn't made a mistake, and that saying goodbye was the right thing to do. Briana guessed it probably was, only it was going to hurt. She'd cry for sure, but then that was part of it, she supposed, letting them see she was sad to leave them.

Oh, how she wanted to stay. Now that she'd thrown it away, she knew that Patrick and Dylan and Fiona and even disaster-plagued Courage Bay were the life she'd have chosen.

Blinking swiftly, she said, "Sure."

She took a turn as catcher, then she pitched for Dylan, who hit the ball into an ornamental fruit tree and proudly climbed up after it.

She had no idea how long they played, but she couldn't stay much later or she wouldn't get on the road tonight. Even worse, she knew Patrick had nothing scheduled for this evening. He might come home early, and she couldn't bear to see him again. Couldn't bear to see that look of contempt in the same eyes that had glowed with love for her only two days earlier.

"Listen, you two, come here. I have to go soon, and I need to talk to you."

They did, and she sat on the grass and pulled them both up against her, one on each side. "How come you're not at work with my dad?" Dylan asked her, and she blinked rapidly.

"I'm not working for your dad anymore," she said, her voice catching.

"Why not?" Fiona asked. "Don't you like my dad?"

"Sure, I like him," she managed to say.

"Me, too." Fiona gave her a big smile. "I love my daddy."

"Oh, sweetie, he's a good man."

"Then why aren't you working for him anymore?" Dylan asked. He had a very logical mind.

"Because I did a bad thing." She sniffed. "I told a lie, and it was very wrong of me."

Fiona nodded and patted Briana's cheek with one hand. "But if you say sorry, Daddy won't be mad anymore. Will you, Daddy?"

Briana started, and turned to follow Fiona's gaze, her face already heating. Sure enough, Patrick was standing just inside the open doorway into the kitchen and he was looking at her. Not with contempt, and not with the blazing love she'd seen two days ago, but with an expression that was...tender.

Fiona ran toward him and he automatically scooped her up, but he never broke eye contact with Briana. And she, like a fool, couldn't look away, even though his image was as blurry as though she were viewing him through old-fashioned glass.

"Hi," Patrick said, stepping forward with Fiona still in his arms.

Oh, God. How much had he heard? "I...I planned to be gone before you got here. Shannon said it would be wrong not to say goodbye to the children."

"Very wrong." He was so close now she could reach forward and use her T-shirt to shine his shoes. Or she could stand up. Dylan scrambled to his feet and she did the same.

Briana couldn't bear to look up past the third button on Patrick's shirt, but she nodded, tears falling yet again. "I'm so sorry, Patrick. I know I don't deserve another chance, but—"

"We told her to tell the truth," Fiona explained to her dad. "So you won't be mad."

"I know that's too much to ask," Briana said, "but I'd like a chance to explain."

He groaned, and she glanced up at him to find the glowing expression she'd believed she'd never see again. "I can't take another explanation. Cecil Thomson explained everything, then Shannon phoned and I got the whole thing again, along with a few helpful insults about my general intelligence. I really think—"

"Shannon called?"

"About two minutes after you got here, if I know my sister."

At that moment, the sister in question, who still hadn't made it back to the fire station, yelled, "Dylan and Fiona, I've got an ice-cream cone with your name on it."

Patrick put Fiona on the ground, and she and Dylan raced for the house.

"I thought she was going to beat me up," Briana said.

"I think Shannon has a far worse punishment in mind," he said, reaching forward and touching her wet cheek. "She wants to stick you with me for life."

Since Patrick's shoulder was so close, and so inviting, and so solid, Briana leaned into it and, for about the twentieth time that day, burst into noisy tears.

"I'm sorry," she sobbed. "I'm so sorry."

"I know," he said, putting his arms around her and hugging her hard. "I should have let you explain last night. But I was too angry, too shell-shocked. To think you could say you loved me and—"

"I did—I do," she managed to choke out. "I wanted to figure out who leaked the story about Uncle Cecil, and then you found the tape, and how could you ever believe I wasn't the evil, manipulative backstabber I seemed. And then I was going to leave, but Shannon said I was running away and made me come and say goodbye to the kids, which was awful, because I love those kids and—"

She stopped for a breath and Patrick was handing her a clean tissue. "I have lots. Shannon supplied me."

Briana wiped her eyes and blew her nose, but somehow she couldn't force herself out of the circle of Patrick's arms. It felt too good to be there again.

Before she could go back to that comforting spot on his shoulder, he tipped up her chin and kissed her, a long sweet kiss that tasted of forever.

"So, you love us, huh?"

She nodded. "I do. I love you. And I love Dylan and Fiona."

"Will you marry us?"

She glanced up and saw the love shining back at her. "I will."

There was a hoot from the open door, and suddenly everyone was hugging everyone else. Briana jumped when something wet and squishy hit her in the back, and she realized Fiona had hugged her with her icing cream cone still in her hand. Oh, well, she figured, if she was going to be their mother, she'd better get used to these things.

Like Dylan kissing her cheek.

And Mrs. Simpson, shaking her hand heartily and telling her about her sister-in-law who was a wonderful caterer and brilliant with weddings.

And Shannon, who snatched back one of the tissues she'd given Patrick to wipe her own streaming eyes, then almost broke every bone in Briana's body when she hugged her.

And Patrick, who said, "By the way, I already found your replacement at work."

"You have?"

"Yep. She brings me sandwiches at lunchtime. You never brought me sandwiches."

Briana laughed. "She sounds perfect."

"You can still transfer to another part of the civil service."

"Okay. But I'm not in that much of a hurry."

"You're not?"

"No. I have a wedding to plan. Fiona? How would you like to be a flower girl?"

"I get to be a flower!" the little girl shouted, spinning in a circle.

"Ring bearer." She drilled a forefinger at Dylan.

A snicker from behind had her turning to jab the air in Shannon's direction. "Oh, no…" Shannon said.

"Bridesmaid."

Patrick laughed richly while his sister shrugged and said, "Love to."

Briana glanced up and caught Patrick's eye and felt her heart flip over. "I love you," she said softly.

He pulled her into his arms and she decided she'd stay there for a while.

Ordinary people. Extraordinary circumstances.
Meet a new generation of heroes—
the men and women of Courage Bay
Emergency Services.
CODE RED
A new Harlequin continuity series continues
April 2005 with

CROSSFIRE
by B.J. Daniels

Armed men take over City Hall.
A woman is shot—and a hostage will be killed every hour if demands aren't met.
SWAT paramedic Anna Carson is going in….

Here's a preview!

THAT DAY at the ballpark, he'd been wearing the T-shirt she'd carried around with her for the last five years. His lucky shirt, he used to call it. Lucky because he'd been wearing it the day he met her.

She normally didn't date his type. Jocks. Stars of one sport or another. The kind of guys her sister Emily always dated. And ended up marrying.

Anna had only given him her number that day at the hospital to shut him up. She'd never expected him to call. If he had called, she would have turned him down. And saved them both a lot of grief. Instead, he'd shown up at the beach, looking sweet and shy and anxious as he asked her to dinner.

And fool that she'd been, she'd said yes. Look where that had gotten them, she thought now, dragging herself out of the memory as Flint halted at the door to the briefing room.

He opened the door and stood back to let her enter.

"After you," she said. "Just one of the team."

He made a face. "Right." He turned and entered the room in front of her.

She braced herself. There were always a few men on a SWAT team who had trouble accepting a woman among them. Fortunately most of the men were younger, more in tune with the times. Flint, she hoped, would prove to be the exception rather than the rule, since the Courage Bay SWAT team was all men.

As she stepped into the briefing room, she heard a male voice ask, "You are aware that the last time a paramedic went in with us, she was injured?"

There was some grumbling agreement.

"That's why I've gone with a paramedic with SWAT training *and* experience," Max answered. "Anna can handle herself under pressure. She knows the danger. She's going to surprise you all."

Anna flushed. "Thank you, Chief Zirinsky," she said, stepping out from behind him to meet a lot of very male faces.

To her surprise, Flint walked over to her side. "Gentlemen, this is Anna Carson, our new SWAT team paramedic. Anna, if you will," he said, giving her the floor.

She looked at the men, then laid it out for them in a flat, no-nonsense account. "I am SWAT trained, second in my class. I spent three years on a Washington D.C. SWAT team. I received medals for bravery and dedication to duty. I have been involved in tactical situations from bank robberies and terrorist attacks to domestic disputes and hostage-suicides." She stopped before adding, "I'm honored to be part of your SWAT team, and I look forward to working with all of you."

Silence, then, "This isn't Washington D.C. We don't have the same kind of manpower." It was one of the older men. His name tag read T. C. Waters. "I, for one, don't like the idea of a woman on the team. Call me old-fashioned—"

"Old-fashioned and a true chauvinist," Flint said, and

laughed. "Welcome to the twenty-first century, T.C. They're even letting women vote nowadays."

"Aw, T.C. even gripes about women reporters on the field during a football game," a younger SWAT member called from the back.

"Yeah, he says he doesn't like the sound of their voices," said another one. More laughter.

"The bottom line here is that Anna's on the team," Flint said, looking over at her. "We treat her like we would any other team member. Forget she's a woman."

There were some chuckles. "Yeah right," one of the guys grumbled. "At least you could have hired an ugly one, Chief."

Even Max laughed this time. The desk sergeant stuck his head in the door. "Chief."

Max went to the door and immediately called Flint over.

Anna didn't have to hear what they were saying. She saw Flint's face, saw the color drain from it and the look he gave her.

His gaze met hers, then moved past to his men. "City Hall. Possible hostage situation. Suit up."